**'You were sa...
lying with y...
bump, and...'**

His voice was deeper and huskier than before,
almost as though he was as affected by the
contact between them as she was.

'And I felt them move,' Sara finished in
a whisper, and saw his eyes flare wide in
response.

'Are you sure?' Now he was staring down at
the curve that was still almost small enough to
be spanned by fingers as long as his. 'Surely
it's still far too early?'

'That's what I told myself,' she agreed. 'But
then it happened again, and a third time, and...
and I thought you would want to know, and...'

Dan drew in a shuddering breath, and she
was stunned to see the bright sparkle of tears
gathering in his eyes.

'Oh, thank you, Sara,' he said, so softly that
she almost had to lip-read the words. 'I can't
tell you how much...'

Josie Metcalfe lives in Cornwall with her long-suffering husband. They have four children. When she was an army brat, frequently on the move, books became the only friends that came with her wherever she went. Now that she writes them herself she is making new friends, and hates saying goodbye at the end of a book—but there are always more characters in her head, clamouring for attention until she can't wait to tell their stories.

Recent titles by the same author:

A MARRIAGE MEANT TO BE
SHEIKH SURGEON, SURPRISE BRIDE
A FAMILY TO COME HOME TO
A VERY SPECIAL PROPOSAL

TWINS FOR A CHRISTMAS BRIDE

BY
JOSIE METCALFE

MILLS & BOON

Pure reading pleasure

First published in Great Britain 2007
Harlequin Mills & Boon Limited,
Eton House, 18-24 Paradise Road, Richmond, Surrey TW9 1SR

© Josie Metcalfe 2007

ISBN-13: 978 0 263 85281 3

Set in Times Roman 10½ on 13 pt
03-1207-48061

Printed and bound in Spain
by Litografia Rosés, S.A., Barcelona

TWINS FOR A
CHRISTMAS BRIDE

CHAPTER ONE

SHE was going to die!

Sara's eyes widened in disbelief as the car headed straight at her in the narrow side street. The headlights almost seemed to pin her in position and she knew in an instant that she would never be able to get out of its path in time.

Instinctively, she took a step back, her foot slipping as it tried to gain purchase on the uneven surface. Her hands flew protectively to her belly to cradle the new life nestling deep inside, a tiny corner of her brain acknowledging the fact that it was far too small to survive even if it were to be delivered by emergency Caesarean.

She heard the car's engine roar suddenly, almost as though its driver had floored the accelerator in direct response to the defensive gesture.

Then, in that final second before the powerful vehicle made contact, it was as if time ceased to exist. She could see everything around her with the pin-sharp clarity of a high-definition photograph—the gleam of the recent rain on the ancient cobbled street; the skinny cat that had been hunting in the gutter for scraps, quickly darting into the safety of the shadows; the harsh glitter of artificial light on expensive automotive paintwork and chrome, and the reflection of her own face in the windscreen where the driver's face should be…her reflection contorted in an expression of rage and… Even as she opened her mouth in a scream of denial the sound was cut off instantly as she was flung aside to land on the unforgiving granite.

She felt a sickening thud as her head struck the kerb with a glancing blow, then the world turned black and disappeared.

'I got the job I was after,' Sara volunteered diffidently into the lull when her vivacious sister finally stopped talking long enough to draw breath.

It was always this way when her shifts allowed her to join the family for a meal. Her mother listened avidly to every scrap of Zara's gossip—about the exotic places she'd been, the fabulous clothes she'd modelled, and the A-list celebrities she'd rubbed shoulders with—obviously believing every word.

Sara had her doubts.

She'd known for many years that every one of her sister's stories was carefully tailored to her audience, regardless of the truth. Even as she listened to yet another tale of her sister's glamorous life her fingertips were taking a well-worn path, absently tracing the line of scarring at her temple that had become the only way she and her twin could be distinguished from each other as children.

The rest of the world had believed Zara's tearful tale of

a childish prank gone wrong. Sara knew better; she had always known that her twin resented the fact that they'd been born identical and that Zara was the younger. The very idea that the injury might have been deliberate was unthinkable and had sickened her, but it had only taken one glimpse of the satisfied expression on her sister's perfect face, when she'd returned home from the accident department with a prominent row of stitches marching all the way from her shaven eyebrow into her uneven hairline, to know the truth.

From that day on, although she'd still loved her sister dearly, she'd never totally trusted her.

'I started the job a couple of months ago...in the accident and emergency department,' she added into the next pause, although no one had been interested enough by her announcement to ask her for further details. Even the father she adored was dazzled by the show his glamorous younger daughter put on for him.

Then a sudden imp of mischief tempted Sara into one of those rare attempts at competition with her sister. Would she never grow out of the childish urge?

'By the way, Zara, there are several rather gorgeous doctors in the department...one in particular is every bit as tall, dark and handsome as that actor who was chasing you a while back.'

The blank expression on her sister's face was enough to confirm Sara's suspicion that Zara couldn't even remember the story she'd told them after her last visit to the United States. In all probability, the rather famously married star hadn't done anything more than smile vaguely in her sister's direction at a crowded party. Then she saw her twin's expression change suddenly into a horribly familiar calculating look and instantly felt sick.

What on earth had made her draw Zara's attention to Daniel's existence? she berated herself the next day when her beautiful sister just happened to arrive at the end of her shift to be introduced to Sara's new colleagues. The last thing she needed was for Zara to turn up flaunting her perfection, especially when Sara was looking her ex-hausted worst at the end of a gruelling shift.

She and her handsome new colleague had quickly dis-covered that they worked well together, but as for their personal relationship, that was still in the fragile early stages, barely beyond the point where she and Dan had admitted that they enjoyed each other's company outside work, too, and wanted to see whether it could develop into something lasting.

Well, that had been as much as Dan had been willing to admit, so far. On her part, she'd known from their first meeting that he was special; that he could very well be the man she'd been waiting for her whole life. There had been something about the gentleness and compassion with which he treated his patients allied with the aura of strength and dependability that surrounded him...to say nothing of the fact that he was probably the sexiest man she'd ever met...

Those weeks of tentatively getting to know each other might just as well not have existed the day Zara walked into the department wafting her signature perfume and demand-ing to be introduced to all her sister's dedicated colleagues.

'Of course, the whole family is so proud of Sara for taking all those exams,' she gushed with a wide smile. 'I certainly couldn't do her job...all that blood and pus and...' She shook her head so that her artfully dishevelled locks tumbled over one shoulder and shuddered delicately.

Sara could have predicted exactly how the ensuing scene would play. From the day that puberty had given her sister that spectacular set of curves, she'd seen it so often before. She didn't need to watch to know that every male in the vicinity was about to make a complete fool of himself as they all vied for one of Zara's smiles, or, better yet, one of the sultry come-hither looks she sent them from under impossibly long dark lashes.

'You didn't tell me you were a twin,' Dan complained as he distractedly delivered the mug of coffee he'd been making for her before Zara's arrival. His eyes were flicking from one to the other and Sara suppressed a wince, knowing just how badly she would come out in the comparison. There was no way that she could compare with such a polished image of perfection while she stood there in crumpled scrubs without a scrap of make-up on her face, especially with her hair dragged back into an elastic band with only a few straggly tendrils to camouflage the worst of the puckered scar that drew her eyebrow into a permanently quizzical arch.

'Hard to believe, isn't it?' she said with a tired smile. 'Have you met her yet?'

She needn't have bothered offering, knowing deep inside that this introduction was the sole reason why her sister was here. In fact, Zara was already undulating her *way across the room towards them in her best catwalk strut, her slender legs seeming endless atop heels high enough to induce vertigo.* Sara felt sick when she saw the intense way her sister's eyes focused on Dan as she drew nearer, almost devouring him piece by piece from his slightly tousled dark hair and broad shoulders to his lithe hips and long powerful legs.

'So, this is the handsomest man in the department, is it?' she purred, all but rubbing herself against him and blinking coquettishly as she gazed up into his amazing green eyes. 'Sara was telling me I just had to come and meet you.'

It was far too late to wish that she'd kept her mouth shut.

What can't be cured must be endured, her grandmother's voice said inside her head, and Sara felt an almost physical wrench as any lasting relationship she might have had with Dan was torn out of her reach for ever. She shut the pain away with all the rest she kept in the box in a dark corner of her soul, and summoned up the appropriate words.

'Daniel, this is my sister, Zara,' she said formally, unable to conjure up even a pretence of a smile. 'Zara, this is Daniel Lomax. He's one of the senior…' She fell silent, realising that she may as well have saved her breath because neither of them was listening to her.

'Hi, Danny,' Zara breathed, and Sara winced, knowing that he hated that diminutive…only this time there was no automatic correction. Well, why would he object now that her sister had both hands wrapped around his arm, blatantly testing his muscles?

She knew how those muscles felt, the taut resilience overlaid with warm skin and silky dark hair. She'd been holding that arm on the way out of the hospital just last night at the end of their shift, delighting in the way his free hand had covered hers to reinforce the fact that he had been enjoying the contact, too.

'If you'll excuse me, I'll go and have a shower and change out of these scrubs,' Sara said, abandoning her untasted coffee as she made a strategic retreat, unable to bear the thought that he might give Zara's hands that same warm caress.

The last glance she threw over her shoulder as she reached the door left her certain that neither of them had even noticed that she'd gone.

Sara woke to a world of pain and noise and eye-searingly bright light. Slamming her lids shut against the unbearable glare, she groaned, unable to decide which part of her hurt the most.

Her hip was agony, but so was her shoulder…and as for her head…

What on earth had happened to her? Had she fallen out of bed in the night? With nothing more than polished floorboards around the new divan it would certainly account for the feeling that she was bruised from head to foot.

'Sara?' said an urgent female voice right beside her ear, but she tried hard to ignore it. It wasn't until she felt the familiar sensation of disposable gloves against her skin as a gentle hand awkwardly stroked the side of her face that she realised that she had an oxygen mask covering her mouth and nose. She tried to turn her head towards the voice but discovered that she was unable to move because of the padded blocks positioned on either side.

She had seen the situation far too many times not to recognise what those sensations meant. She was strapped to a backboard with her head and neck restrained because of the fear of exacerbating a spinal injury.

'Sara, can you hear me?' the voice said over the cacophony of bleeping monitors and voices snapping out orders. 'Sara, love, you've had a bit of an accident and you're in the hospital…' And with those few words terror gripped her. Suddenly she remembered everything that had happened to her in excruciating detail.

The car appearing in the narrow road just as she started to cross it on her way back to her flat…the brightness of the headlights as it came straight towards her…as it hit her and sent her tumbling to the ground…deliberately?

Then she remembered something even more important.

'My baby…!' she keened, her voice muffled behind the oxygen mask, panicking when she was unable to move her hand to her belly, so desperate to know by the familiar feel of the gentle swell that it was still safely inside her.

Then she heard the echo of what she'd said and guilt hit her hard. 'The baby,' she said, deliberately damping the forbidden emotions the way she'd been forced to right from the first day she'd had the pregnancy confirmed. 'Is it all right? Has anything happened to the baby?'

'Stay still, Sara,' ordered the familiar voice of the senior orthopaedic consultant. 'You know better than to move until we've taken spinal X-rays and checked them.'

'No! No X-rays!' she gasped, feeling almost as if she was trapped in a terrifying nightmare. 'I'm pregnant! No X-rays!'

'Hush, sweetheart,' said a softly accented voice, just another of those voices that she'd only recognised in the guise of colleagues before. Everything was so very different now that she was the helpless patient; they were her doctors and nurses and they would decide what treatment was best for her. 'You just lie there and trust Sean O'Malley to know how to take an X-ray without harming your child,' he said, coming to stand in exactly the right place so that she could see his familiar freckled face and carroty curls and the sincerity in his bright blue eyes. 'I promise you on my word as an Irishman that the wee angel won't come out glowing in the dark.'

Sara gave a hiccup that was part laughter, part sob and somehow found a smile. 'I trust you, Sean O'Malley,' she whispered, knowing absolutely that a man who delighted in every one of his four rambunctious red-headed sons would never do anything to risk anyone's child, let alone a colleague's.

The one voice she didn't hear, even though it seemed as if every last member of the A and E department was crammed into the resus room around her, was Daniel's.

What sort of irony was that? she mused silently, a tear tracking from the corner of her eye into her hair and stinging as it reached the place where her head had come into contact with the granite kerbstone. The one person she wanted beside her as she tried to cope with the terror, the one colleague who had the most to lose if anything happened to the child she was carrying—and he wasn't there for her.

'You're late, Sara,' her mother scolded, almost dragging her into the house as soon as she set foot on the doorstep. 'You could at least have tried to get here on time for your sister's big announcement.'

'Sorry, Mum,' she apologised automatically as she shrugged out of her voluminous jacket. 'Where's Zara going this time? Or is it a contract with one of the really big fashion shows?'

'Oh, Sara! You're not wearing that old thing again! You could at least have made an effort.' This time there was a sharper edge to her mother's voice as she saw what her daughter was wearing. 'I really don't understand why you always look such a dowdy mess. No one would ever believe that the two of you were identical twins.' She flung up her hands in despair as Sara glanced down at her favourite black trousers teamed with the soft ivory blouse that she usually wore with it. It had always been enough for a family supper before, so what was different tonight?

Then her mother opened the door into the lounge and she heard the buzz of conversation that could only be made by several dozen voices and froze.

'Mum? Is there a party or something?' she demanded, hanging back. She was suddenly horribly conscious that she hadn't bothered putting any make-up on after her shower and had done nothing other than run a brush through her hair either.

'Sara, you know very well that your sister and Danny

are making their big announcement this evening,' her mother snapped as she beckoned her with an insistent hand. 'She rang you up and told you all about it more than a week ago and everyone else has been here for hours. We've only been waiting for you to arrive.'

'Dan…?' Sara felt her eyes widen as the implication hit her with the force of a wrecking ball.

Zara and Dan?

A big announcement that her sister had told her about?

For just a moment she thought she was going to be sick, but with her mother's hand now firmly clamped around her elbow she had no choice but to enter the room beside her as she pushed the door wide.

The room seemed to be crammed with people, every one of them dressed to the nines in their most elegant finery, but the glittering butterfly in their midst, effortlessly out-shining them all, was Zara.

So why was it that the first pair of eyes she met were the luminous green ones that belonged to Dan…eyes that only had to glance in her direction to double her pulse rate and send her blood pressure into orbit no matter how serious the medical emergency they were working on.

Hastily, she dragged her gaze away, knowing that she couldn't afford for anyone to guess just how much it was costing her to keep herself together while her world fell apart around her.

This was the first time that she'd seen her sister since the day that she'd turned up in A and E to be introduced to Dan, and when she'd heard nothing more, Sara had dared to breathe a sigh of relief. Even if they had gone out together, Zara's attention span was notoriously short and she was certain her fickle sister would soon tire of an escort who would never be at her beck and call.

She was so confident that the two of them hadn't hit it off together after all that she'd actually been contemplating screwing up her courage to ask Dan out for a drink later in the week, hoping that the two of them could continue the relationship they'd embarked on when she'd joined the department, longing to see where it would lead them.

The last thing she'd expected was that he and Zara had been carrying on a whirlwind courtship that would result in an engagement. Zara hadn't dropped a single hint...and she certainly hadn't phoned her a week ago to invite her to their engagement party.

It was a good job that she'd had years of practice at hiding her feelings from her manipulative sister. Even so, she needed a moment or two to compose herself, grateful for the time it took for her mother to walk across the room to join her father. Then he tapped the edge of his glass to attract everyone's attention. He beckoned Zara and Daniel to join the two of them in front of the fireplace before he cleared his throat portentously.

'Friends,' he began.

'Romans and countrymen,' added one of Zara's modelling friends with an inebriated giggle, only to be hushed by one of the older, more sober guests.

'Friends, as you all know, this is a very special occasion,' Frank Walker began again as Zara finally met Sara's gaze and she saw that, oh, so familiar smug expres-

sion followed by a cuttingly dismissive glance from head to toe that told Sara as clearly as anything that her sister had deliberately neglected to tell her about the purpose of this evening's gathering for exactly this reason.

If ever there had been a moment that demonstrated how different the two of them were it was this one, with Zara...flawless, beautiful Zara...the centre of everyone's admiring gaze while she was purposely relegated into the background, not even afforded the courtesy call that would have allowed her to look her best. No one would be left in any doubt why Dan would choose Zara over her dowdy, less-than-perfect twin.

'Audrey and I are delighted to welcome you all this evening to celebrate the engagement of our beautiful daughter Zara to this handsome chap here.' There was a muted cheer and happy laughter from a small group who could only be Dan's family—not that she'd ever had the chance of meeting them before. 'In case you haven't heard all about him yet, he's Dr Daniel Lomax, and I have no doubt at all that he'll soon be a consultant in emergency medicine at one of the top hospitals in the country. So, I'd like you all to raise your glasses to wish them both every happiness. To Zara and Danny!'

With all the glasses being raised and the voices echoing her father's words, the fact that she hadn't been given a glass shouldn't have been noticed, neither should the small detail that she was totally unable to utter a word, her eyes burning with the threat of tears. But Zara noticed, and once more smiled like the proverbial cat that had got the cream.

Then Daniel noticed too, his slightly dazzled expression replaced by a puzzled frown when he caught sight of her standing alone just inside the door with her hands hanging heavily by her sides.

Then Zara noticed the focus of her new fiancé's attention and put an immediate end to it, reaching up to cup his cheek with a hand that glittered with a million points of fire as the light caught her engagement ring, then she leaned possessively against him to give him a prolonged kiss that had the room hooting encouragement and left him branded with her scarlet lipstick.

This time when her gaze met Sara's from the circle of Daniel's arms her expression screamed just one word—mine.

'Relax. The baby's fine,' soothed the technician as she slid the probe through the gel on the pale curve of Sara's exposed belly. How few weeks ago it had been that she'd celebrated the fact that she was actually beginning to look pregnant. 'Look, Sara, you can see the heart beating for yourself and there is absolutely no sign of an abruption or any other sort of a bleed in there. Now, did you want me to print an extra copy for you? I might even be able to get a shot that tells you whether you're having a—' Her cheerful patter halted abruptly as she leant forward to take a closer look at the screen then moved the probe to change the angle of the view. 'What on earth…?' she muttered under her breath.

'What? Rosalie, what's wrong with the baby?' Sara demanded, the pain in her head intensifying with her fear for the life of the child. 'Is it something to do with the accident? Was the baby injured or…?'

'Not at all! There is absolutely nothing wrong with your baby,' the young woman announced as she turned with a wide grin on her face. 'In fact, there's nothing wrong with either of them. Look, Sara…it's twins! There are two heart-beats!'

Suddenly, Sara didn't know whether to laugh hysteri-cally or cry. As if her life wasn't in enough of a tangle already. Now she was going to have to tell everyone that it wasn't just one baby she was carrying but two. Both sets of future grandparents would be ecstatic, without a doubt, but Dan would be the only other one in the family who would understand just how much more perilous this preg-nancy had become.

As if thinking his name had finally conjured him up, there he was, standing in the doorway with an expression Sara had longed to see on his face for so long…concern for her welfare. Or was it, as ever, concern for the preg-nancy?

'What on earth have you done?' he demanded as he strode in, grabbing her case notes as if he had every right to examine them, and she realised that nothing had changed. Any concern he felt was obviously for his pre-cious offspring.

Disappointment made her headache even fiercer and lent an acid edge to her tongue.

'Don't worry, *Danny*, the baby's fine. In fact, you could even say you're getting a genuine bargain—buy one, get one free.'

'What on earth are you talking about?' he snapped, and turned towards the startled woman standing in front of the high-tech control panel. 'Has she been concussed?'

'No, I'm not concussed,' Sara insisted before Rosalie could even draw a breath to answer, completely ignoring the fact that she'd apparently been unconscious among a stack of soggy cardboard boxes for the better part of half an hour before anyone had found her after the accident. 'In fact, according to everybody, I've been extremely lucky. My foot slipped on the wet cobbles as I tried to turn away from the impact to protect the baby, so I only sustained a glancing blow from the car.' She ticked her injuries off on her fingers, a slightly difficult feat with one arm strapped across her body.

'I've had a couple of stitches and got a goose egg on my forehead and I'll probably end up with one or even two black eyes; I dislocated my shoulder, but that's been put back where it belongs—hence the strapping; my hip is black and blue where it hit the granite cobbles, but even without X-rays of the region the orthopaedic consultant's almost certain I didn't break anything there and he says the cracked fibula should heal without any complications. Oh, and apart from that, I feel as if I've lost several yards of skin from various portions of my anatomy.'

She'd been glaring at him throughout her recitation and couldn't help feeling a little remorse when she saw the colour swiftly drain from his face. Not that she intended letting him off the hook. After all, it wasn't Sara, the person, that he was worried about, it was Sara, the person who had been systematically browbeaten by her family into agreeing to carry a surrogate baby for Dan and her inexplicably infertile sister.

'So, let's get to the really good news,' she continued bitterly, with a gesture towards the image frozen on the screen between them. 'Exhibit A is the scan that not only confirms that there is no evidence of injury to the brood mare's procreative organs, but also the fact that she's carrying not one but two babies. Congratulations, Dannyboy! You hit the jackpot first time!'

And even though it brought tears of agony to her eyes to force herself to turn away from him, she made herself to do it, unable to bear looking at those heart-stopping green eyes any longer.

'Are you sure you don't want to change your mind about the pain relief?' Rosalie murmured, startling Sara into the realisation that the young woman was still standing there. She'd been so focused on her acrimonious conversation with Dan that for a moment she'd completely forgotten that there was anyone else in the room with them. Not only had the technician heard her swiftly muffled groan of pain when she'd turned away from the man but she'd had a ringside seat for every word that had gone before it. Now, the fact that she was pregnant by her sister's husband would be food for gossip right around the hospital.

'Hasn't anyone given her any analgesia yet?' Daniel exploded, confirming her suspicion that he was still standing behind her…still gloating over the image of his children, no doubt.

'I don't want any unnecessary drugs,' she snapped. 'I

used the Entonox while they put my shoulder back and stitched me, knowing that was safe for the baby…oh, excuse me, *babies*. I'm quite capable of deciding for myself if I want or need anything else. Now, please, go away and leave me alone. Shouldn't you be off duty by now? Zara will be waiting for you,' she added pointedly.

That thought caused a different pain altogether and was nearly enough to persuade her to accept the drugs on offer. The idea of wiping all the agony away with a swift injection was growing more attractive by the moment. After all, if she was unconscious, she wouldn't be able to think… wouldn't have to try to unscramble the images inside her head, the impossible images that were trying to tell her that it had been her own sister who had tried to run her down in that narrow side street.

CHAPTER TWO

'SARA! How could you be so clumsy? Your dress is ruined!'
her mother exclaimed in horror as she followed her into
her hotel bedroom.

Sara hid a grim smile of satisfaction as she unceremoniously stripped the torn dress off and kicked the revolting
garment towards the bin in the corner of the room. Even
in a crumpled heap in the shadows the colour was offen-
sive and from the first horrified moment she'd seen it she'd
realised exactly why her sister had chosen it, and had been
determined to thwart her plan. Even if today was her
sister's wedding, she had no intention of being made a
laughing-stock in front of all their friends and family...and
especially, she admitted guiltily, in front of Dan.

'I'll just have to step down from being a bridesmaid,'
she said logically, putting Plan A into action even as her
mother hurried across to retrieve the expensive dress to
examine the extent of the damage. It wouldn't be nearly so
hard to stand in the background while she tried to hide her
emotions from everyone else; to hide the fact that she desperately longed to be the one standing beside Dan—the

man she loved—exchanging their vows. Zara was the twin accustomed to standing in the limelight and putting on the face that the rest of the world expected to see. 'It won't take me long to put my smart suit on,' she continued, refusing to think about anything beyond the immediate situation. 'I'll catch up with the rest of you downstairs before the ceremony starts.'

'You can't!' her mother wailed, wringing her hands. 'You've got to be Zara's bridesmaid. You're her only sister…her twin! What would everybody think?'

'Does it really matter what they think?' Sara asked with her head in the wardrobe, already reaching for the black silk suit she'd chosen as an elegant alternative to the burnt-orange meringue her sister would have had her wear.

The thing that had amazed her was that her mother had apparently been oblivious to what had been going on right under her nose while the attendant's clothes had been chosen for the wedding party. She'd commented approvingly about the clever idea of a colour theme graduating from the creamy ivory of the bride's dress through various shades of gold and topaz for the dresses her wraith-thin modelling friends would wear, but how could she not have seen that both the colour and the style Zara had decreed for Sara's dress were an abomination that did absolutely nothing for her second daughter's colouring or more rounded shape?

And as for the hairstyle… Sara's eyes flicked towards the mirror, her glance taking in the simple severity of the swept-back style that would have complemented the fine lines of her face if it hadn't also revealed the imperfection of the scar her sister had inflicted on her so long ago.

The fact that her mother was oblivious to everything but that things should be exactly as her beautiful daughter wanted was an old hurt that was unlikely to go away any time soon.

There's none so blind as them that will not see, she could hear her grandmother say darkly, and Sara smiled, remembering that the indomitable old woman she'd adored had been one of the few who had seen straight through Zara. Granny Walker had been the person who had always known when her younger granddaughter had been practising her wiles and had taken no nonsense, especially when Sara had been the butt of Zara's machinations.

'You're not wearing black to your sister's wedding,' her mother pronounced as she whipped the hanger out of Sara's hand and angrily flung the contents onto the bed. 'There must be something we can do with your dress. It's a designer original. The man did it specially...as a favour to Zara because she's his favourite model.'

Sara knew without question that there was no way she was ever going to be able to wear that dreadful dress again. She'd made certain of that when she'd decided exactly what damage she was going to do to it. As far as she was concerned, everything about the dress was proof that the designer must have detested her sister...maybe even the whole female half of the world's population.

'How about this?' she suggested as she switched to Plan B and took out the dress that had been hanging in the wardrobe just waiting for the right moment. 'I was going to change into this after the photos. Do you remember it?

It was an evening dress of your mother's, from before
Nana married Granddad. I thought that if I wore it for part
of the day, it would be almost as if she were here, too.'

The dress was simplicity itself and while the fluid silk
looked nothing special draped over a hanger, once she was
wearing it, the rich honey-coloured fabric was so supple
that it looked as if it had been poured over her curves with
a delicate hand.

'Oh, darling…' As she'd hoped, her mother caught her
breath at the sentimental idea and when she reached out
a tentative hand to stroke the fabric, Sara knew that she
had won the first skirmish.

'Shall we see if it fits me well enough?' she suggested,
already knowing what the answer was going to be—the
dress fitted her as if it had been made for her. This battle
plan had been worked out in every detail, knowing that it
was the only way she was going to outwit her spiteful
sister. 'I remember you told me once that my hair is exactly
the same colour as Nana's was.' Unlike Zara's, which had
been lightened season by season until it was now at least
half a dozen shades paler than Sara's dark blonde.

Her mother was quite misty-eyed as she helped Sara
into the substitute dress, trying not to disturb either her
hair or her make-up, and when she stood beside her in
front of the mirror and had to resort to biting her lip so
that she wouldn't cry and ruin her own mascara, Sara
knew that the battle was won. There was just the matter of
teasing out a few 'accidental' tendrils of hair to camouflage the twisted line of scarring that pulled her eyebrow
up at an angle…

'*Whatever you do, don't catch this one on the doorhan-dle,*' *her mother warned with a sniff into her lacy handker-chief as she bustled towards the door.* '*I'll just go and make sure that everyone else is ready. Zara's hairdresser was just putting the finishing touches once her veil went on when you had your accident. We don't want to keep dear Danny waiting any longer.*'

With those few words, the taste of victory over what she would wear was ashes in Sara's mouth. What did it matter how much better she looked in her grandmother's dress, or that her ugly scar was hidden? Dan probably wouldn't even notice she was there; he wouldn't have eyes for anyone other than his beautiful bride.

Zara looked like a flawless life-sized porcelain doll, Dan thought as he pushed open the bedroom door and found her lying on their bed.

It was hardly surprising that she'd fallen asleep. He was hours later than usual tonight, but he just hadn't been able to make himself leave any sooner. The thought that Sara might be stubborn enough to insist on going home, even after such a potentially fatal encounter, had found him hanging around until he'd made certain that she had agreed to spend the night in hospital and was settled into a side ward.

He smiled wryly when he saw how perfectly Zara was posed. It was as if she was expecting her favourite photographer to start clicking away, her hair spread artistically over the pillow and one hand draped elegantly over the edge of the bed. It would almost have been a relief to find

her curled up in an untidy ball with creases on her face
from the pillow. As it was, sometimes it felt as if he was
married to a mannequin, with her face always perfectly
made up and never a hair out of place, even on the increasingly rare occasions that they made love.

The heavy sigh took him by surprise and the weight of
regret that accompanied it made him feel very guilty.

He'd realised almost as soon as he'd placed the ring on
Zara's finger that he'd made a dreadful mistake, but by then
there had been no way out.

Even if he *had* divorced his new wife, he'd known that
there was no way that Sara would have stepped straight
into her sister's shoes…what woman would, especially
after the way he'd treated her?

He might only have met Sara a few months earlier, but
they'd already admitted to a mutual attraction and had
been exploring the possibility of a long-term relationship.
For the first time in his life, he'd even found himself wondering about the possibility of marriage in the not-too-
distant future.

Then he'd met Zara and discovered the meaning of the
words 'whirlwind courtship', his feet hardly seeming to
touch the ground before he'd found himself engaged and
caught up in the planning of an uncomfortably high-profile
wedding.

Up to that point, their relationship had been conducted
largely in secret—at Zara's insistence that she didn't want
to chance the media intruding—so he hadn't really noticed
that she was such a favourite with her parents. It had only
been after their marriage that he'd noticed just how little

her family regarded Sara, in spite of the fact that she was now a qualified and highly proficient doctor in a busy A and E department. All their pride was definitely focused on their glamorous, vivacious, younger daughter.

In a strange way, he could even understand it, to a certain extent. He'd certainly been blinded by Zara's lively attractions when she'd set out to captivate him. What man wouldn't have been flattered to have such a stunning woman hanging on his every word in such an ego-stroking way?

How could he not have realised that she was all outward show with very little substance beneath it? Why had it taken him so long to recognise that Sara was worth a dozen of her self-centred twin?

Well, there was nothing he could do about it now. He was married, and even though he knew it had been one of the worst decisions of his life, he was not a man who broke a promise, so he certainly wouldn't go back on a solemn vow. He would just have to be content with the fact that Sara had agreed to carry a child for the two of them...two children, in fact, he recalled with a sudden surge of the same incredulous delight that had swamped him when he'd learned of it. Although how Zara would respond when he told her that she would shortly be learning to cope with being a mother to not one but two newborn babies...

'Zara?' he called softly, stifling a sigh of resignation. His wife was not going to be in a happy mood when she saw how late it was, even though it had been her sister's welfare and that of the babies she carried that had caused the delay. She was almost fanatical about preserving her looks with adequate sleep and certainly didn't like eating at this hour. 'I'm sorry I'm late, but it was unavoidable. Your sister had a rather…' He broke off with a puzzled frown.

She hadn't so much as stirred, even when he'd lowered himself wearily to the edge of the bed. Something rustled as it slid to the floor between the side of the bed and the cabinet—a letter she'd been reading before she'd fallen asleep? Perhaps it was a glamorous new contract she'd wanted to gloat over while she'd waited for him to come home?

He reached out and touched her hand…her curiously lifeless hand.

Suddenly, he switched into doctor mode as all the hairs went up on the back of his neck in a warning that something was seriously wrong.

'Zara!' he called sharply as he leant forward to take a closer look at the silent figure. He'd been standing in the doorway wool-gathering for several minutes and only now was he noticing that she was so completely still that she didn't even seem to be breathing.

'Zara, wake up!' he ordered harshly, his fingers automatically searching her wrist to find a pulse. 'Zara!' He heard the panic bouncing back at him from the expensively decorated bedroom walls when there was no sign of any rhythm under his fingertips. Was that because his ordinarily rock-steady hands hadn't stopped shaking from the moment he'd heard that Sara had been knocked down? Frantically, he probed her slender neck and breathed a sigh of relief when he felt the reassuring throb of the artery under his fingertips.

It was slower than it should be...much slower...and her skin felt cold and clammy. It was no wonder that he hadn't been able to see her breathing because her respiration was so shallow as to be almost imperceptible.

But at least she *was* breathing and her heart *was* beating, so that gave him precious time to try to make a diagnosis so that he could help her survive whatever had happened to her.

But first...

'Emergency. Which service do you require?' said a crisp voice in his ear as he continued to make his examination, trapping the phone in position with one shoulder.

'Ambulance,' he said tersely. 'My wife has had some sort of collapse. Her pulse and respiration are both depressed and her pupils are fixed and dilated.' He managed to give the operator his address even as he reeled with horror at the possibility that Zara was imminently going into cardiac arrest.

Without some secure means of administering oxygen and the supplies to set up an IV line he had no way of improving her tidal volume or boosting her systolic pressure above 80. At the moment it must hovering around 70 because her femoral pulse was barely perceptible. If it dropped below 60 the carotid pulse would disappear, too, and she would be just minutes away from irreversible brain damage and death...

'Come on! Come on!' he urged as he transferred her swiftly to the floor and began carefully controlled cardiac compressions to boost the volume of blood going to her brain, desperate to hear the sound of a siren drawing closer.

The weight of his guilt was almost crushing as he kept automatic count inside his head. If he'd come home when he'd said he would, rather than hovering over Sara and waiting till she was settled in her room, would he have arrived in time for Zara to tell him that she was feeling ill?

Would he have been able to prevent her collapsing in the first place?

A sudden hammering on the front door made him realise that he'd completely forgotten to release the catch for the ambulancemen to get into the flat.

'She's in here,' he directed as he quickly led the way back to the bedroom and dropped to his knees beside her again. 'Her systolic must have been close to 70 when I found her because her femoral pulse was barely palpable and her pupils were fixed and dilated.' He glanced across at the man who dropped to his knees on the other side of the body to begin his primary survey, and they came face to face for the first time.

'Dr Lomax!' the paramedic exclaimed, clearly shocked to see him, but he immediately became the consummate professional. 'Do you know what happened to her, sir?' the paramedic asked as he bent over the ominously still figure between them to check her pulse and respiration rates for himself.

As he did so, Dan heard the man's foot strike something to send it skittering under the bed but no one even bothered to glance at it. At the moment nothing mattered more than giving Zara a chance to continue her vibrant life.

Out of the corner of his eye Dan saw the man's colleague depositing an oxygen cylinder on the carpet and he reached out for it, leaving him free to set up the defibrillator with the swift ease of much practice.

He was ashamed to see how badly his own hands were trembling as he fumbled to tighten the mask against her face, blocking out the heart-stopping thought that Zara might already be in need of the defibrillator's violent charge to reset her heart rhythm. It was several horrified seconds before he remembered that it could also be used as a valuable monitoring and diagnostic tool.

'I've no idea what happened to her,' he said, dragging his thoughts back to the question he'd been asked, frustrated when he saw that the man was having trouble finding a vein. But, then, with her blood pressure so low, it was hardly surprising. Still, he had to fight the urge to take over and do the job himself. They needed to get the IV started and the lactated Ringer's running into her veins as soon as possible to get her blood pressure up. If she'd had some sort of spontaneous bleed that had caused a catastrophic drop in her blood pressure…

'I came home from work to find her lying on the bed,' he continued, forcing himself not to waste any time second-guessing, even as the need to do *something* urged him to continue CPR. 'At first, I thought she was sleeping, but when I tried to wake her…' he shook his head in disbelief. 'That's when I realised how ill she was.'

'Do you know if she'd had any alcohol to drink before you found her?' he asked, and Dan almost smiled.

'It's unlikely. She never drinks anything stronger than a white wine spritzer…too many calories,' he added.

'Do you know if she's taken any drugs, sir?' the young

man asked as he peeled the gel pads from their protective backing and positioned them swiftly on Zara's chest, and even though Dan knew that the questions were necessary for him to do his job, the suggestion shocked him.

'No!' he exclaimed immediately, horrified at even the thought that this bright beautiful woman might have wanted to kill herself. Then he remembered a conversation he'd overheard at one of the parties she'd dragged him to earlier on in their marriage. He'd been shocked to learn just how many of her fellow models resorted to chemical assistance to maintain their almost skeletal slenderness.

'Oh, God,' he muttered, praying that Zara hadn't been tempted down that route. In a profession that valued the freshness of youth above almost everything else, her age was already counting against her. Had she been that desperate to extend her modelling career that she would use drugs to help her compete with all those younger wannabes?

'I don't know,' he admitted finally. 'I've never seen her taking anything, but…'

'Could you go and have a look in the bathroom, please, sir,' the paramedic asked firmly, as he gestured to his colleague to take his hands off their patient while he activated the machine to monitor the state of her heart. 'We'll take over here now.'

'Stand clear. Analysing now,' said the disembodied voice programmed into the machine as he strode into the *en suite* bathroom, almost grateful for an excuse not to watch if they were going to have to make her beautiful body convulse with the brutality of a shock.

It took precious seconds to search through a mirror-fronted cabinet crammed full of beauty products of every shape and size, but the only tablets he could find were those in a half-full plastic bottle of over-the-counter painkillers.

'No shock required,' the voice was advising as he came back into the room, and his heart lifted briefly at the thought that at least Zara hadn't gone into ventricular fibrillation or cardiac arrest.

'Did you find anything, sir?' prompted the paramedic as he rejoined them and he saw that in his absence they'd intubated Zara to secure her airway, rather than relying on the face mask, and had connected her to their portable oxygen cylinder. The monitor clipped to her finger was already starting to record an improvement in the saturation level in her blood.

'No drugs, other than some generic analgesics,' he said, disorientated by the fact that he was little more than a bystander in a situation where he was usually the one in charge. But this was completely different to working in A and E. There, he could work fast and effectively, treating any number of cardiac arrest patients in a single day with his brain working swiftly and clearly and every possible piece of equipment readily to hand.

Here, it felt as if his thoughts were travelling through treacle as he saw the paramedic's gloved fingers sort through the pre-loaded syringes in his kit. Somehow, he just couldn't get his brain to tell him what the man should be looking for, or why.

'They were paracetamol and the bottle was half-full,' he added, before the man could ask.

'What about the bedside cabinet?' prompted the other man, and Dan dragged his gaze away from what the two of them were doing to stride across and pull the drawer completely out. He upended it over the bed and several items fell off the edge of the mattress and hit his foot to land out of sight under the bed.

'Some herbal sleeping tablets and…a bubble pack of contraceptive pills,' he added in disbelief, suddenly wondering just how many kinds of a fool he'd been. So much for Zara's grief that she couldn't give him a child! If she'd been taking contraceptives to prevent herself getting pregnant, had anything about his marriage been real?

He reached under the bed to retrieve the items that had fallen, his first sweep revealing nothing more than a couple of pens and the locked diary that Zara had written in each night.

His second sweep shocked him to the core.

'Barbiturates!' he exclaimed when the empty bottle rolled into view and he caught sight of the name of the contents printed on the label. 'Where did she get barbiturates from?'

There was an awful silence in the room, with only the soft sibilance of the oxygen to break it, all three of them gazing at the slender beauty with varying degrees of disbelief, incomprehension and pity. They all knew that the incidence of barbiturate overdose had dropped considerably with the introduction of newer, safer sleeping tablets, but if the label on the bottle was genuine, the dangerously addictive drugs were clearly still readily available in other parts of the world to globe-trotters such as models.

Although why *Zara* would feel the need to take…

'We need to get her to hospital quickly, sir,' the para-medic said briskly, as he selected several syringes. 'Do you know your wife's approximate weight so I can give her the first dose of sodium bicarbonate?'

Thank goodness he'd found the prescription bottle, he thought, realising wryly that he was probably one of very few husbands who would know almost to the ounce what his wife weighed, the result of Zara's obsessive morning ritual had been a cause for alternating delight or despair for every single day of their marriage.

At least they now knew precisely which barbiturate she'd taken and that it was one that bicarbonate would promote more rapid urinary excretion—anything to get the drug out of her system before it could do any more damage. Zara was already deeply comatose and if he'd arrived home any later…

He shook his head, deliberately shutting that thought away as he followed every move that the two-man crew made with critical eyes. Not that he doubted their compe-tence. From the moment they'd entered the flat they hadn't made a false move.

His colleague had already piled everything else back into their packs and as soon as it was closed he straight-ened up. 'I'll get the stretcher,' he announced and took off out of the flat.

'Do you want to travel with her, sir, or—?'

'I'll follow you,' Dan interrupted, and understood the look of relief that briefly crossed the man's face. He didn't know many paramedics who would be entirely comfortable about doing their job under the eagle eyes of an A and E doctor, especially when the patient was a member of that doctor's family.

Apart from anything else, he and his colleague were probably wondering at the situation between Zara and himself that could have led her to make such a desperate gesture.

He sighed heavily with the realisation that there was no way this would remain a secret, no matter how strict the rules were over patient confidentiality.

'The last thing any of us needs is speculation and gossip,' he groaned under his breath as he followed the stretcher out of the flat and paused just long enough to make sure the front door had locked behind him. It was going to be hard enough to tell Zara's family that she had made an attempt at taking her own life without the whole hospital speculating what went on behind closed doors.

If that was what it had been, he continued agonising as he followed the flashing lights through the busy traffic, the urgent scream of the siren an audible reminder that the outcome of the situation was far from certain.

Suicide? Zara? It still seemed impossible. Had she just intended to give him a scare? Had it only been the fact that he had been late that had made this such a serious situation, the extra hours giving the drugs so much more time to do their damage.

And if she…*when* she survived? He hastily altered the words inside his head, feeling a renewed stab of guilt that he could even contemplate the alternative.

Anyway, he thought heavily, as far as her health was

concerned, no one could predict how well or how badly she would recover. Only time would tell how much permanent damage the drugs had done to her system.

The fact that she was his wife was another matter entirely. Zara wasn't anywhere near as important a model as she pretended to be, but any speculation that it might somehow be *his* fault that she'd come so close to death could start a media feeding frenzy that would ruin all their lives, to say nothing of his career. The lower end of the tabloid market would have the whole situation blown out of all proportion the minute they heard that she'd taken an overdose, especially if they unearthed the fact that the two of them had resorted to a surrogate pregnancy.

He followed the flashing lights all the way to the emergency entrance, his brain rerunning everything that had been done to try to stabilise Zara's condition. He was so preoccupied that he only just remembered in time to pull into the designated staff parking area rather than cluttering up the area around the emergency entrance.

As his feet pounded across the tarmac towards the emergency doors, the lights cast long shadows that made it seem as if the doors never got any closer, but finally they slid silently open in front of him.

'Dan? What on earth are you doing back here?' demanded his opposite number on the night shift, but he didn't even slow his pace, his long strides taking him unerringly through to the resuscitation rooms at the other end of the department.

'Dan! Come in,' called the consultant already standing the other side of Zara's ominously still body, his face creased in concern as he beckoned him into the room.

For a moment, as he shouldered his way through the doors, Dan was filled with dread. Had things got worse during the ambulance journey from his flat to the hospital? Zara's condition had been so serious that he was hardly likely to look across the clinically stark room and find her sitting up and preening herself in front of any males in her audience, but if the bottle of barbiturates she'd taken had been in her body too long, it was all too likely that she might never come out of the coma.

As he stared across at her, she looked even more like a porcelain doll under the unforgiving fluorescent lights, with an almost waxy sheen to her skin.

He slumped back against the wall and watched in awful fascination as his superior did everything *he* would have done if she were one of his patients, from aspirating her stomach contents to remove any tablets still undigested, to trying to neutralise any drug-laden fluids with activated charcoal before they could be absorbed by her body.

This just couldn't be happening, he thought, his helplessness making him feel sick to his stomach.

Zara had so much to live for, and before this he would have sworn that she was far too self-centred and conceited to ever think of suicide. Why on earth would she do something so…so…?

'I'm sorry, Dan,' the consultant apologised, and Dan knew that he was going to confirm his worst fears…*life extinct*.

Just the thought of those solemn words was enough to change the way he saw the woman who was his wife. Somehow her slenderness became mere gauntness without the aura of her vivacity, her expert make-up smudged into a caricature of its usual perfection and her shimmering blonde hair artificial and brassy.

He closed his eyes to try to block out the images, unable to look at her any more.

How *was* he going to break this latest news to her family? It had been bad enough when he'd been contemplating the best way to tell them that Sara had been knocked down, but *this*...

'We're going to have to put her on IPPV,' the consultant warned when a monitor suddenly shrilled a warning that her oxygen saturation was falling dangerously low in spite of the mask. Dan's eyes flew open and he blinked in disbelief. How had he managed to convince himself that Zara was dead when the room was filled with the sound of all those monitors?

'Her respiratory effort is so badly depressed by the drugs...' his superior continued, almost apologetically.

'It's OK,' Dan reassured the man, immeasurably relieved that all was not yet lost. 'Just do what you have to do. You don't have to talk me through every step. I trust you.'

More than he would trust himself at the moment, he admitted silently. The whole scene seemed totally unreal, especially coming so soon after Sara's narrow escape. How many disasters could one family cope with in a single evening?

At least he'd given in to Sara's request not to inform her parents what had happened to her. He'd been reluctant, knowing how excited they were about the pregnancy, but

Sara had promised that she would go straight to them when she was released in the morning, confident that hearing about the accident would be far less traumatic if they could see with their own eyes that she was perfectly all right.

Well, more or less, he temporised, imagining just how badly bruised she must be after such an event. Her pale skin would soon be all the colours of the rainbow, and as for the pain…that must be considerable, especially as she'd refused any further analgesia.

His respect for his sister-in-law couldn't have been any higher, as a colleague, as a person and as the temporary mother of his children. Sara might not always get along with her twin—an understandable case of sibling rivalry, perhaps?—but she'd certainly proved how much she loved her sister by putting herself through the traumas of a surrogate pregnancy.

Behind his closed lids he saw a flash of another image—that of two tiny hearts beating side by side. And he could picture equally clearly the fiercely protective emotions in Sara's eyes. It had been obvious just how much it had meant to her to see the babies for the first time and to know that her accident had apparently left them untouched.

A secret regret hit him afresh, one that he'd been living with for several years now.

He knew that he'd behaved stupidly when Zara had set out to entice him, had already realised, even then, that Sara had been more than halfway in love with him. He'd probably been heading in the same direction until her sister had started her determined pursuit.

And he'd been stupid enough to be flattered and intrigued by the prospect of being desired by a woman so confident in the power of her beauty. Had it been the fact that she was the twin of someone to whom he was already attracted that had made him believe he had been in love with her?

Enough!

Enough rationalisation! Enough excuses! Whatever the truth had been then, now was a different matter entirely.

He straightened his shoulders and deliberately opened his eyes to gaze directly at the woman he'd married, confronting his blame head on.

It had been his responsibility to protect her, and he'd obviously failed if she hadn't felt able to come to him with her problem—be it depression or a dependency on drugs. He had no idea when it had started or how long it had been going on…no idea whether her brush with death had been an accidental overdose or a deliberate one.

No doubt the police would have to be involved and would doubtless grill him at length about the state of his marriage.

How much worse would it have been if she'd died while he'd been hovering around Sara until she had been settled on the ward?

As it was, even if she did recover fully, it would be some time before Zara was in any fit state to answer questions. He certainly had no idea what had made her take this drastic action, so if the police needed to know why she'd done it, they would probably have to interview Zara's friends and colleagues as well.

'She's stable now, so we're transferring her up to ICU,' the consultant said, and Dan suddenly realised just how much time had elapsed while he'd been lost in his thoughts.

His superior patted his shoulder reassuringly, but there was something else entirely in the expression in his eyes, something that didn't need to be put into words. They both knew that there was no guarantee of a happy outcome.

'I've sent samples up to the lab, just to confirm what she'd taken to make sure we've done all the right things,' he said quietly, then added, 'Give them half an hour or so to get her settled up there,' exactly the way *he* would have done had she been one of *his* patients.

'How long before we know…? How badly is she…?' He couldn't finish a single question, knowing there were no real answers.

'I'd love to be able to tell you that she's going to be all right,' the consultant said, patting Dan's shoulder again. 'But you know as well as I do that only time will tell. Shall I leave it to you to contact the other members of her family, or would it be better coming from me?'

'I'll do that now,' Dan said, his voice sounding almost rusty as it emerged from a throat tight with too much emotion.

How *was* he going to break the news to Zara's doting parents?

CHAPTER THREE

SARA heard the all-too-familiar swoosh and creak of the door to her room as someone pushed it open, and barely managed to stifle a groan.

Not *another* member of staff preventing her from sleeping! There couldn't possibly be an inch of her body that hadn't been examined, poked and prodded…or had a needle stuck in it.

When nothing happened after several seconds of silence, she opened cautious eyes, wondering what was going on. Seeing Dan standing beside the bed, gazing down at her, immediately doubled her pulse rate, then she realised that the oversized gown she'd been given had slipped right off one shoulder. She had to stifle a groan of agony when she tried to hike it back into a more modest position with the wrong hand.

'Dan?' she croaked, trying for impatient but only managing to sound pathetic. 'I thought you were going home. You don't need to keep checking up on me, too. There's an army of nurses doing that every two minutes and…' She had to bite her tongue to stop herself delivering another tirade when she still owed him a massive apology for the first one. He'd come to see her just after she'd had her ultrasound scan to see if she and the babies were all right and she'd jumped right down his throat. It just wasn't fair that she was taking all her fear for the babies out on him.

'I didn't come to check up on you,' he said quietly, one hand going out to the chair beside her bed, then pausing.

It was almost as if he wasn't sure whether to stand or sit, and if it was sit, whether it should be on the chair or on the side of her bed. The whole incident took no more than a few seconds but it was totally uncharacteristic of a man who was usually decisiveness personified.

Finally, he perched uneasily on the edge of the bed, his lean hip nudging against her bruised thigh…not that she would say a word. Secretly, she still revelled in every occasion that he was close to her…close enough to smell the clean soapy scent of his skin and see the tracks where his fingers had raked through his hair. Close enough to see the lines of strain that had grown deeper still since she'd seen him just an hour or two ago.

'Dan? Is something wrong?' Panic struck her and her hand flew to cover the precious duo nestling deep inside her. 'Is it something to do with the babies? Has something shown up on one of the tests?'

'No!' he exclaimed, clearly startled. 'I'm sorry, Sara, I didn't mean to frighten you. As far as I know, everything's still fine.'

'So, what's wrong?' she demanded. 'I can tell you've got something serious on your mind and… Is it Mum and

Dad? I *told* you not to tell them about my accident. I was going to go and visit them as soon as I'm set free in the morning, so that they could *see* that I'm not—'

'It's not your parents,' he interrupted, then sighed heavily and shook his head. 'Sara, I'm sorry but there's only one way to tell you this. When I got home this evening, I found Zara unconscious. She'd taken an overdose of barbiturates.'

'Barbiturates?' she gasped, reeling. 'No! Not Zara. She wouldn't.' It was her turn to shake her head at the impossibility of what he was suggesting. Her sister might be selfish and egotistical but she wasn't anyone's fool. She'd seen far too many of her fellow models slide down the slippery slope of drug addiction, hooked when the desire for impossible slenderness came with an intoxicating high. With a few high-profile exceptions she'd seen it ultimately ruin their careers as model agencies and advertisers alike crossed them off their books.

Anyway, barbiturates were usually prescribed for people having difficulty sleeping, so they wouldn't be any use to someone wanting to get high. Deliberate overdoses were usually confined to people who were depressed and that definitely didn't sound like her vivacious sister.

'There was no name on the bottle and the drug name was generic…possibly bought abroad or over the internet…and the bottle was empty when I found it on the floor beside her,' he said quietly, and she could see from his expression that he was already blaming himself.

'How long ago…?' she began, only to halt in mid-sentence as a sudden thought struck her. If Zara had been at home, taking an overdose, then her crazy suspicion that it had been her own sister driving the car that had run her down this evening must have been just that…crazy. Unless she'd gone home after she'd done it and taken the drugs in her remorse…but, no, that didn't make sense either. Nothing made sense. Not the fact that she'd been absolutely certain that it had been Zara behind the wheel of the car that had deliberately aimed at her, or the fact that she would have access to barbiturates or would deliberately take an overdose.

'She was in a pretty bad way when I found her,' he said, answering the question she would have asked if her brain had been working well enough to formulate it. 'She was already comatose, her breathing and pulse rate both depressed, but when her stomach was pumped, there were a fair number of undigested tablets, so she must have taken them some time this evening.'

Sara's relief that her sister couldn't have been responsible for her accident faded with the realisation that there would still have been plenty of time for her to have returned home and swallowed the drugs before Dan had found her. But that begged the question: why would Zara do it, especially when Sara was expecting the child… *children*…that she'd begged Sara to carry for her?

'Have you told my parents?' Sara could only imagine the state her mother must be in, knowing that her beautiful perfect daughter had…

'Not yet. I had to come and tell you first,' he said simply.

Pleasure that he'd wanted to break the news to her *before* notifying his in-laws flowered inside her, only to wither to dust when he added, 'I didn't want you to get a garbled version if the news reached you through the hospital grapevine.'

That was more like the Dan she'd been working with for the last couple of years—logical and practical. Of course there hadn't been a personal reason why he would have wanted to give her the news in person. When was she going to stop searching for traces of the connection they'd made when they'd first met? When was she going to come to terms with the fact that any feelings he'd had towards her had vanished the instant he'd met Zara?

'Where is she? What treatment is she receiving? When can I visit her?' she demanded briskly, forcing herself to be equally logical and practical. She tried to push herself up in the bed and fell back with a groan when every muscle and joint complained.

'You're in no fit state to go anywhere yet,' he growled as he carefully slid one arm under her shoulders and effortlessly lifted her up, supporting her while he positioned the pillows behind her.

Sara shivered. Every tiny hair had suddenly stood up in reaction to the warmth of his arm surrounding her. Not that her hospital room was cold. If anything, it was far too hot. But somehow it was different when it was Dan's body heat in a wide swathe across her back where his strong arm held her, and as for the soft wash of his breath stirring her hair against her face and neck…

'But…' It was hard to get her thoughts in order when he was so close. Thank goodness they never did any more than brush against each other when they worked together, or she'd never be able to do her job properly. Still, she didn't dare to take a full breath until he laid her gently back against the pillows and released her to step back a little from the bed. The last thing she needed was another lungful of that familiar mixture of soap and musk to contend with.

'Sara, I'll let you know as soon as they say she's stable enough for visitors,' he promised, his green eyes darkly serious. 'At the moment she's so deeply unconscious that she wouldn't even know that you were there, and you wouldn't be doing yourself any good either. You need to give your body time to heal.'

'But you're going to have to tell Mum and Dad tonight, aren't you…about Zara, I mean?'

'And that means I'll have to tell them about what happened to you, too,' he pointed out.

'No! *I'll* tell them, when I—'

'Sara, think about it,' he interrupted. 'They're going to want to see you…they'll be *expecting* to see you when they arrive at the hospital, waiting outside ICU until Zara's consultant allows you in to see her.'

'But…' She closed her eyes in defeat. He was right, of course. And she wasn't in any fit state to be sitting around in the little relatives' room all night.

'Which would you rather—that they knew that you'd been involved in an accident or that they thought you couldn't be bothered to be with them when they need you?' he challenged, and she slumped back against the pillows, knowing that she couldn't argue against that sort of logic.

'You will tell them that the babies are OK, won't you…?

Oh!' she exclaimed with a shadow of her usual smile. 'They don't know that it's twins yet!' She groaned as she tried to reach into the bedside locker for the precious picture of the scan. 'Could you get the photo for me, so you can show it to them?'

'Actually…' He paused a second and she was startled to see a soft wash of colour sweep across the lean planes of his cheeks as he reached into his pocket to take his wallet out. 'I hope you don't mind, but I asked the technician to print an extra copy.'

For Zara. Of course.

'I should have thought of that…to get one for the two of you. After all, they're going to be *your* babies, so you actually have *more* right to a picture than I do.'

'Sara, don't,' he said swiftly, and startled her by trapping her hand in the warmth of his, the green of his eyes darkening as they gazed intently down into hers. 'I can't imagine how difficult the whole process is for you, but you have every right to a picture of the babies that are developing inside you. I'll never be able to thank you enough for what you're doing. An extra picture of an ultrasound scan is nothing in comparison.'

His sincerity was obvious and actually managed to soothe some of the ache that had been filling her heart ever since she'd been persuaded along this path. The last thing she'd wanted to do was carry the children of the man she loved, only to have to give them away. The fact that he genuinely seemed to appreciate the sacrifice she was making was like balm to her soul. All she had to do was make sure that he never had any idea of her true feelings towards him.

* * *

It had been every bit as dreadful as he'd thought it would be, Dan thought wearily as he propped himself against the wall of the ICU waiting room several hours later.

Unfortunately, it had been his mother-in-law who had answered the door of their smart suburban home, and when she'd realised that Zara hadn't been with him, something in his face must have told her that he was the bearer of bad news.

'She's had an accident, hasn't she?' she wailed. 'I *knew* something must have happened. I just knew it! I've been waiting all evening for Zara to call to let me know she'd returned home safely. I told her she should have asked you to drop her car off at the garage.'

As he ushered her through to her smartly decorated lounge, trying vainly to calm her down, a small corner of Dan's brain registered the odd snippet of information. What had been wrong with Zara's car that it had needed the attention of a mechanic? Both their vehicles had only recently been serviced.

'What's the matter? What's going on?' his father-in-law demanded gruffly from his favourite seat at one end of the settee. He fought to fold the newspaper that had spread itself across his lap and tried not to look as if he'd fallen asleep in front of the television.

'Our Zara's had an accident!' his wife keened. 'I told her she shouldn't be driving in London traffic. Danny should have looked after her. *He* should have taken her car to the garage if there was something wrong with it.'

'Is that true, lad? Is she hurt? How bad is it?' Frank might not be so openly emotional as his wife but it was plain that he was immediately worried about his precious daughter.

'Can we sit down?' Dan suggested, still uncertain just how much he should tell them. The results hadn't come back from the lab by the time he'd left the hospital, so he still wasn't certain what level of concentration the drugs had reached in Zara's body and what that would mean for her prognosis. If they had depressed her respiration and starved her brain of essential oxygen long enough to cause permanent…

'She's *dead*! My baby's *dead*!' Audrey cried hysterically, and for a moment he almost relished the idea that he might need to slap some sense into the woman.

'No! She's *not* dead!' he contradicted firmly, hoping that he sounded more confident than he felt. He took hold of both her shoulders and guided her until the backs of her knees met the edge of the settee and she collapsed next to her husband. 'Neither of your daughters is dead,' he said firmly, desperately praying that he was telling the truth.

'You mean, something's happened to *Sara*?' Frank demanded. 'But I thought… I'm confused. Did Zara ask you to come and tell us? Why didn't she come herself, or is she staying with Sara?'

'Is it something to do with the baby?' his wife demanded sharply. 'Zara will be *so* disappointed if anything's wrong with…'

Between the two of them he was having a hard time getting a word in edgeways. It looked as if he was going to have to abandon any idea of breaking things to them gently.

'Sara was knocked down by a car this evening as she

was walking home from work,' he announced bluntly. Too bluntly? he wondered when it looked as if the pair had stopped breathing.

'No!' He should have known that their mother would recover the power of speech first. 'Oh, Danny…how? Oh, tell me she hasn't lost Zara's precious baby.'

'She was knocked unconscious, her leg was broken and she's badly bruised, but she had a scan to see if she had any internal injuries—'

'She didn't have any X-rays, did she?' Audrey demanded sharply. 'I don't want my first grandchild being born deformed because it had X-rays.'

Not a word of concern about the injuries *Sara* had suffered, Dan noted, even as he had to stifle a smile when he remembered Sean O'Malley telling him just how fiercely Sara had objected to having X-rays. He could just imagine that she'd been the very picture of a lioness defending her cub.

'Actually,' he said, sidestepping the issue of X-rays entirely to focus on the news that still sent his spirits soaring, in spite of all the trauma of the last few hours, 'the scan showed us something we weren't expecting to see— that Sara's carrying twins.'

The momentary silence had a completely different feel this time, but even as they began exclaiming in delight he despised himself for his cowardice. He should be telling them about the much more urgent situation confronting their younger daughter.

His reprieve was all too brief.

'What did Zara say when you told her?' his father-in-law demanded with a beam. 'I bet she was delighted.'

'Well, I was very late getting home, after making sure that Sara and the babies were going to be all right,' he began, even as a voice inside his head jeered at him for trying to assuage his guilt for arriving home so much later than he'd intended. The outcome would have been very different. 'I thought she was asleep, but when I went to tell her the news, I couldn't wake her and had to call an ambulance to take her to hospital.'

'Hospital?' his mother-in law shrieked in disbelief. 'Zara's in hospital, too? Why? What's the matter with her?' She began to struggle to her feet, slapping viciously at her husband's hand when he tried to stop her. 'I've got to go to her straight away. *You'll* have to take me,' she declared with a glare at Dan.

'Why wouldn't she wake up? What's the matter with her? Do you know?' Frank demanded, clearly dumbfounded by the news.

'It looks as if she's taken an overdose of drugs...barbiturates,' he said, and was nearly deafened by the howl of denial.

'*Drugs!* That's a lie! My Zara wouldn't touch the filthy things.' Audrey was sobbing with rage now. 'Why would you say such a dreadful thing about your own wife? You should know she's the most beautiful, most perfect—'

He ignored the start of the familiar litany, interrupting bluntly. 'The bottle was found beside her, and some of the drugs were found still in her stomach when we got her to the hospital and pumped her out.'

'But—' Frank began, but as ever his wife's voice overrode his tentative attempt.

'Then you got them all out and she's going to be all right?' she demanded shrilly, in spite of the fact that her certainty about her daughter's convictions had been summarily destroyed. 'Did she tell you why she took them? It must be a mistake…a…a…'

'They pumped out as many as they could, but she'd already absorbed enough to send her…' At the last moment he paused, wondering if the mention of the word 'coma' would be the final straw. Instantly, he knew that his mother-in-law would definitely have hysterics if he so much as mentioned the possibility, and sidestepped the prospect by choosing a less emotive word.

'Zara's deeply unconscious, so she's been taken into Intensive Care where she'll be monitored constantly until the drugs wear off and she wakes up.'

He hoped they were too shocked to notice the guilt he was trying to hide, but no way was he mentioning the very real chance that the drugs might have already caused significant damage. He knew that, as her parents, they had a right to information about their daughter, but he was hoping that he wouldn't have to be the one to tell them. It was bad enough that *he* knew that Zara might never wake up again, at least not in any meaningful way.

It might be cowardly, but he was intending to leave it to the consultant to tell them that, even when the effect of the drugs she'd taken did wear off, the daughter that the two of them idolised might already be lost to them for ever.

Sara was a different matter. There was no way he could

have left her to find out what her sister had done, not after the shock her system had already sustained this evening.

He stifled a weary sigh as he assisted his sobbing mother-in-law into his car, knowing that there would be very little chance that he would be seeing his bed tonight.

Hoping that his silence could be taken as the result of navigating the busy streets, he tried to get his thoughts in order.

He would definitely have to contact Human Resources as soon as possible to notify them that he wouldn't be in for his shift the next day…or for the foreseeable future, at least until the drugs had left Zara's system and he had some idea what sort of prognosis they were looking at.

He would also have to see if there was a relatives' room free for the Walkers to use. He couldn't imagine that anyone would be able to persuade Audrey and Frank to leave the hospital until their daughter was out of danger, but they might be persuaded to rest in between the short visits they would be permitted by her side.

Then there was Sara.

Bruised, bloodied and broken her body might be, but her spirit appeared even stronger than ever if the way she'd confronted him was any gauge.

He found himself stifling a grin when he remembered the way she'd turned on him like a spitting cat. It was the closest she'd ever come to telling him exactly what she thought of him, although he had a pretty good idea.

He'd barely admitted to himself how much of his time had been spent thinking about her, even in those first few weeks. Then he'd been stupid enough to allow himself to be snowballed into marriage with her sister, committing the oldest blunder in the book when he'd allowed his hormones to overrule his heart.

Then, when he and Zara had been unable to conceive, he'd been amazed and delighted when his in-laws had told him that Sara had volunteered to act as a surrogate mother for them.

How stupid could he have been? He should have known that her parents' desire to give Zara everything she ever wanted would have made them resort to any means to persuade her soft-hearted sister to agree.

No wonder she had so little time for him, even when he was concerned about her welfare. No wonder she'd been convinced that his only interest was that his child had been unharmed.

Children, he reminded himself with a surge of mingled joy and terror.

He'd been amazed and delighted to see not one but two hearts beating strongly on the ultrasound screen, evidence that they were both still snugly ensconced in their rightful environment and supremely unaware of their narrow escape. One side of him was ecstatic to see the evidence that his precious children weren't just a dream but a miraculous reality. It was the other side—the doctor side of him—that knew enough to be afraid; the doctor half of his brain that knew just how much more dangerous the existence of that second baby was, both to the pregnancy and to Sara herself.

Bearing a child was already one of the most danger-ous things a woman could put herself through, and to carry twins…

He shook his head when he realised that he was already planning a session on the computer to access all the relevant statistics, irrespective of the fact that knowing the figures would worry him even more.

'What's the matter?' Audrey demanded in a panicky voice as she entered the relatives' room at exactly the wrong moment. 'Why did you shake your head? Did the doctor say something to you while we were in with Zara? She's not going to…? Oh, no! Please! She can't die. Not my beautiful girl!'

Dan swore silently as her voice rose shrilly with every word, his head thumping unmercifully.

'No one's told me anything,' he said firmly as he took her by the shoulders and leant down to force her to meet his gaze. 'Audrey, the only time I've spoken to Zara's consultant was when you were with me. The situation hasn't changed. We've just got to wait and see how her body copes with whatever it is she's taken. We've just got to be patient.'

'How *can* I be patient?' she demanded angrily, shrugging his hands off and whirling away. 'I'm her *mother*! You have no idea how dreadful it is not being able to do anything. Just waiting…'

'You could visit Sara,' he suggested. 'She must be wondering what's happening down here, worrying about—'

'If she were that worried she'd be here with us,' Audrey interrupted sharply. 'I can't believe how selfish that girl is, to be lying in bed when she should be down here with her sister…with us…'

'Sara's in no fit state to go anywhere,' Dan snapped,

rapidly reaching the end of his tether. It was unbelievable that parents could be so concerned about one of their daughters and so dismissive of the other. They seemed to care so little for Sara and were so unappreciative of her and everything she'd achieved that it bordered on emotional abuse.

It certainly wasn't something that he would ever do to *his* children. His heart missed a beat when he visualised the flickering evidence of those two tiny beings that would one day look up to him and call him Daddy. It was an awesome responsibility and he would make certain that they both knew that their father loved each of them as much as the other.

'Mum? Dad?' said a hesitant voice from the doorway, and Dan spun on his heel, his eyes widening with disbelief when he saw the shaky figure sitting in the wheelchair.

The bruises on her face looked livid and angry already, especially against the stark white of the dressing covering her stitches. He could only guess how many other injuries were hidden under the back-to-front gown she wore as a wrap, but nothing could hide the ungainly cast stabilising her broken leg.

'Sara!' He strode towards her when he saw her struggling one-handed to propel herself further into the room, her face so pale it seemed almost bloodless. He didn't know whether to be angry with her for being crazy enough to make the journey when every inch of the distance between her room and ICU must have been agony for her, or proud that her determination was enough to bring her here in case her parents needed her support.

All he knew was that he was suddenly filled with an overwhelming need to protect this valiant woman from anything that might cause her any more pain.

CHAPTER FOUR

DAN was still seething when he finally took half an hour to race home for a shower and a change of clothes.

'Those parents of hers are unbelievable!' he growled as he leaned wearily against his front door, almost too tired to make his way to the bathroom.

He was sure his mouth must have gaped when there hadn't been any evidence of sympathy at the shocking extent of Sara's injuries, not a single word of concern that she must have escaped death by the merest whisker, to say nothing of the possible loss of their grandchild…grand-*children*, he corrected himself and felt that crazy grin creep over his face again, banishing his bad mood at a stroke.

He reached for his wallet and extracted the precious image printed from Sara's first scan and awe joined his feeling of delight. Not one but two tiny beings were still growing safely inside her womb, in spite of their close brush with death. He could still feel that first surge of emotion when he'd seen the image of their minuscule hearts, the beats so rapid that they'd almost seemed to flicker on the screen.

'My babies,' he whispered as he outlined their precious images with a visibly trembling fingertip and was shocked to feel the hot press of tears behind his eyes.

This…*these*…were the one good thing that had happened in such a very long time. These two tiny beings made everything worthwhile.

Even the knowledge that your wife is lying dangerously ill in ICU? asked a disapproving voice inside his head. That brought him up short for a moment and guilt struck him hard that he was feeling such delight while Zara's health—her very life—hung in the balance.

His shoulders slumped still further when he realised that even though her situation was serious, with no guarantee for a happy outcome, he found it strangely hard to care any more than he would if Zara were just another patient brought into A and E in the course of his working day.

'That certainly took the smile off your face,' he muttered as he strode across the lounge towards the bathroom with the weight of a very long day pressing down on his shoulders again. At the last moment he veered towards the mantelpiece to prop the precious image in full view, torn between the desire to replace it in his wallet to keep it close to him and the equally strong need to keep it safe.

His first step inside the bedroom was like a punch to the gut. He and Zara were both reasonably tidy people so it was a real shock to be confronted with the shambles that remained from his efforts to keep her body functioning until the paramedics arrived.

The bedclothes straggling onto the floor were mute testimony to the way he'd hastily pulled her down onto the firmer surface, and there certainly hadn't been time to straighten anything up before he'd leapt in his car to follow the ambulance to the hospital.

He stepped forward and reached out to gather up the bedding then let it fall again, unable to find the energy to care that the bed needed making or, more to the point, the inclination to sleep in it at all when he thought about what had so nearly happened there.

He needed sleep. In fact, if he was honest with himself, he was nearly out on his feet with exhaustion, both with the stresses of a long hard shift and then the double shocks of first Sara's and then Zara's admission to hospital. Even so, he couldn't face the thought of climbing into that bed, not when he didn't know whether its last occupant was going to survive.

He nearly fell asleep standing under the shower, the fierce pummelling of the water jets on the back of his neck and across his shoulders almost as blissful as a massage.

Not that he'd had the time or inclination for massages recently. In fact, not since the last time Sara had taken pity on him in the very early days of their fledgling relationship.

'Don't go there!' he groaned aloud, but that did nothing to stop the images playing through his head.

It had been a rough shift, not unlike the last twelve hours, and he'd made the mistake of sitting down at the table in the staffroom rather than going straight home. The next thing he'd known had been Sara's voice in his ear, calling his name and waking him to the realisation that he could barely move his neck for the crick in it.

'Can I see if I can get rid of that stiffness for you?' she'd offered, and for a moment he hadn't been certain which stiffness she'd been talking about. Waking up with her soft voice and the warmth of her breath in his ear had matched perfectly with the dream he'd been having, and both had had a predictable effect on his body.

Her fingers on his neck and shoulders, alternately stroking then firmly kneading only helped his neck and shoulders. His other reaction he'd had to keep to himself until he'd returned to his bachelor digs with images of persuading Sara to join him there as soon as possible playing in his head.

Had there been a hormonal overload in his system at the time, because it had been just days later that he'd met Zara and been completely bowled over by her blatant interest in him…so different to Sara's more reserved manner and so flattering to the male ego.

The steam followed him out of the shower as he padded through to the wardrobe with nothing more than a towel wrapped around the back of his neck.

He was operating on auto pilot now, knowing that he needed clean clothes and to put something in his stomach and knowing that his duty was to support his in-laws while they waited impatiently for the scant five minutes in each hour that they were allowed to spend at their daughter's bedside. It was so wearing to sit with them knowing that they were pinning their hopes on finding a dramatic improvement each time they went in.

He was already running on his reserves and knew he needed to sleep, and sleep soon, but somehow…somehow he couldn't think about sleeping while Zara's condition was unresolved and especially while Sara was valiantly sitting with her parents, waiting for better news. She had worked just the same killer hours as he had and had then suffered the trauma of being run over.

The clean shirt made him feel a bit less ragged and he was just reaching for some bread to toast to fill the gaping hole where his stomach should be when his pager shrilled.

'Daniel Lomax,' he said, his heart in his mouth by the time the phone was answered in ICU and he was switched through to the consultant's office. He wasn't on duty but had told the ICU staff he was taking his pager home with him if they needed to contact him.

'Daniel, I thought you'd like to know that we've had another set of results back from the lab and—'

'I'm on my way, sir,' Dan interrupted, when he heard the strange note in the consultant's voice. Suddenly he knew that something was wrong, and a surge of adrenaline instantly banished his exhaustion. 'I'll be there in about eight minutes,' he promised, already halfway out of the door as he ended the conversation.

By the time he reached the street he'd fought his way into his jacket and had his keys and phone safely in his pocket. The rain was still lashing down and for a moment he considered going round the back of the flats for his car, then shook his head. The flat had been chosen because of its proximity to the hospital but the security system protecting the cars from opportunist thieves would take longer to get through than if he ran. Nothing was going to interfere with getting to ICU as quickly as possible.

He was soaked to the skin and so wound up that he was shaking by the time he made it up the last flight of stairs.

'What's happened?' he gasped as he reached the interview room, one of the nurses having pointed the way as soon as she'd seen him.

'It's good news!' Audrey exclaimed with tears in her eyes. 'They've found out that Zara *hadn't* taken an overdose of barbiturates after all. I *told* you she wouldn't. She's not into all that drugs nonsense.'

'Not barbiturates?' Dan said with a frown, turning towards Mr Shah. 'But the bottle was on the bed beside her when I found her. I don't understand.'

'It's possible that it was some sort of…' he hesitated a second and threw a glance in Audrey and Frank's direction. 'A decoy of some sort, to make you think she'd taken something else.'

'Well, it worked,' Dan said flatly, hating the thought that even in something as serious as an overdose of drugs Zara was playing stupid games. 'So what *had* she taken?'

'The lab results say that the majority of the tablets were paracetamol but there was definitely some phenobarbitone, too.'

'See!' Audrey exulted, obviously completely oblivious to the serious expression on the man's face. 'It was nothing more than some over-the-counter tablets. We'll soon have her home again, good as new.'

'We knew in A and E that there was something wrong when her stomach was pumped,' Dan said, remembering his shock when he'd seen just how many tablets there'd been. It had looked like handfuls of them still largely undissolved, to say nothing of the ones that must have already dissolved and entered her system. 'The label on the bottle meant it should have been capsules but they were bringing up plain white tablets.'

'Well, it looks as if she thought she was taking just enough phenobarbitone to send her to sleep, and miscalculated. She's still comatose.'

And that wasn't the worst of it, Dan knew with a sinking feeling, already working out for himself what Mr Shah was going to tell them next.

'She was given activated charcoal when she was brought into A and E after her stomach was pumped,' he recalled with a feeling of dread.

'Unfortunately, not long after the IV was set up, she had an adverse reaction to the antidote we were giving her,' the consultant said, obviously trying to keep things simple for Frank and Audrey. 'We've given her antihistamine to dampen the reaction but, because she's had the charcoal, methionine won't be an effective alternative.'

To say nothing of the fact that she was still unconscious and would be unable to swallow the methionine tablets, Dan added silently. He'd been horribly right in what he'd feared. 'That means you're going to have to start the same IV again at the lowest possible infusion rate so you don't trigger the reaction for a second time.' And *that* meant it would take that much longer before the drug in her body was rendered harmless—time in which it could be doing untold damage to her liver and kidneys, especially to someone who was borderline for malnourishment, the way so many fashion models were.

'So, how long will it be before she wakes up?' prompted Audrey eagerly. 'How long before we can bring our little girl home?'

The consultant sent Dan a wry look, sharing the knowledge that here was yet another set of parents who were only hearing what they wanted to hear.

'We're giving her medication to mop up the drugs still in her system, but everything else is largely up to her own body. She won't wake up until the sleeping pills she took have worn off, and we have no idea how long that will take. It's just a case of waiting,' he explained kindly, and Dan knew that the man had recognised that neither of his in-laws was capable of taking in the possibility of any other outcome. As far as they were concerned, Zara would wake up as quickly and easily as though she'd fallen asleep in front of the television the way she sometimes did after a long flight.

'Excuse us,' Frank said suddenly, getting out of his seat after a quick glance at his watch. 'It's our time to go and sit with Zara. We wouldn't want to miss it.'

'By all means,' the consultant said, getting up courteously to open the door for them. He glanced back at Dan as though asking whether he wanted to leave, too, but he didn't move. There were so many more questions he needed to ask, particularly about the lab results and the level of concentration of the paracetamol that had been found in Zara's blood.

At the last moment, just as the door swung closed, he caught sight of a slight cotton-clad figure in a wheelchair out in the corridor.

'Just a moment, sir,' he requested, and hurried across to open the door again, to find Sara making her laborious way towards her sister. Her parents must have passed her just seconds ago but had clearly left her struggling on her own.

'Sara,' he called gently to attract her attention, and stifled a wince when he saw how gingerly she turned her head towards him. She shouldn't be wheeling herself about when she was so badly bruised. She should be lying in bed, giving her body time to heal.

'Did you want to have a word about Zara?' he invited. 'The latest lab results are in.' He glanced over his shoulder to find that the consultant hadn't been quite so quick to mask his reaction to Sara's injuries. 'Do you have any objection if she joins us, sir? Zara is her twin, but Sara is a doctor on the staff here, down in A and E.'

'I've no objections at all. Come in, my dear. Let me hold the door for you.' He hurried to hold the door wide while Dan strode out to take hold of the handles and provide the propulsion she needed. 'My word, your family *is* in the wars. What on earth happened to you?' he asked as he gently shook her hand as though afraid she would shatter.

'A hit-and-run accident on my way home from work,' she said, as she used her hand to shift her cast to a more comfortable position, the wry smile that she sent him doing nothing to lift the evidence of pain from her face.

Dan ached for her, wishing there was something he could do, but there was no one on earth who would be able to persuade her to take painkillers if she'd decided against them.

'How bad were the results?' Sara asked quietly, as ever

going straight to the point. 'How much damage has she done to herself? I suppose she got the barbiturates on one of her foreign trips.'

'Actually, my dear, it's not the barbiturates that are causing the biggest problem,' Mr Shah explained. 'The majority of the drugs your sister took were paracetamol.'

Dan wouldn't have believed that Sara could have gone any paler until he saw it happen. Her lips were almost colourless and she had to lick them with a flick of her tongue before she could speak.

'So, she's on IV N-acetylcysteine? What concentration has the paracetamol reached? Is it still rising or is it on the way down now?'

'It's not rising any more, but it hasn't started dropping yet,' the consultant said apologetically. 'As you say, we put her on IV NAC, but she quickly developed side effects. We've had to administer antihistamine and drop the dosage of the drip right down.'

The small frown pleating her forehead told Dan that she had worked out for herself the reasons why they couldn't use the alternative antidote, and admired the fact that her brain was still working just as fast as usual in spite of everything that had happened over the last day.

'Also,' Mr Shah continued inexorably, 'we have no way of knowing how long the drugs have been in her system. If it is only a short time—less than eight hours—then it will not be such a big problem, but we cannot assume anything.'

Dan was watching Sara's face as the consultant was speaking, so he saw the sudden widening of her eyes and the deepening of her frown. The expression must have pulled her stitches if the wince and the protective hand that came up to cover the dressing was any indication.

For a moment it was obvious that she was conducting some sort of internal debate and the way her hazel eyes darkened told him it wasn't a pleasant one. Then her hand dropped to the curve of her belly in a protective gesture as old as time and panic roared through him. Was she in pain? Was she suffering a delayed reaction to her accident? Was she miscarrying?

'Sara,' he began, fighting for self-control when all he could think of was the precious picture propped on his mantelpiece, 'is everything all right? Are you feeling—?'

The sudden sound of a hasty knock at the door cut him off as the consultant excused himself before calling, 'Enter.'

'Mr Shah, Zara Walker seems to be waking up. Did you want to—?'

'Thank you. We will come now,' he said swiftly, already pushing back his chair. 'Do you want to follow me?' he threw over his shoulder, but didn't wait for a reply as he hurried out into the corridor.

'Here, let me. It'll be quicker,' Dan said as he took over the propulsion of her wheelchair, leaving Sara to slump back into the seat.

She must be really close to the end of her tether, he realised when he saw the slump of her shoulders. Zara might be the professional model but Sara had an innate elegance and style of her own and poor posture wasn't a part of it.

'Are you sure you're all right?' he asked, taking advantage of the fact that there simply wasn't enough space for the wheelchair in Zara's room—there were just too many people in there at the moment. 'For a moment, back in the interview room, you looked…worried. Is it the baby? You're not having contractions, are you?'

'*Babies,*' she corrected softly. 'And, no, I'm not having contractions, thank goodness. I was just…' She paused for a moment, then shook her head. 'No. It's nothing.'

'Are you sure?' Some sixth sense was telling him to press her. 'If it was something that could possibly help Zara…'

There it was again, a look of indecision, as though she couldn't bring herself to say something…detrimental about her twin. He had no right to insist that she speak to him and was still trying to find a way to persuade her to trust him with…well, with whatever it was putting that frown on her face when an all-too-familiar voice called his name.

'Danny?' it quavered, but whether the weakness was real or feigned he wouldn't like to hazard a guess. It could just as easily be either, knowing Zara. 'Is Danny there?' There was a plaintive note this time and he had to stifle a wry smile. Now certainly wasn't the right time to question Sara, but he was definitely going to make a point of it before he left the hospital this time.

'I'm here, Zara,' he confirmed lightly, straightening up so that she could see him above the general mêlée of medical staff and her parents. Her vital signs had already been checked and if he wasn't mistaken, there was more blood being drawn for another lot of tests to track the progress of the antidote.

'Come closer, Danny,' invited Audrey, beaming widely and beckoning with the arm not wrapped around her precious daughter's shoulders. 'Look! Isn't it wonderful? Our Zara's back with us as good as new. Isn't she beautiful?'

Zara had been born beautiful, Dan thought dismissively. It was all on the surface, not something she'd had to work for…unlike Sara's medical qualifications.

Zara's initial expression when her mother drew her attention to him was one of open delight, then her wide hazel eyes drifted to one side as though she was trying to see what had attracted his attention away from her at such an important moment.

He took a step aside so that she could see her sister sitting in the wheelchair beside him. He was totally shocked when, instead of an expression of concern or, at the very least, an equally welcoming smile for her sister, her look was one of…what? It was definitely more than horror at the fact that she'd suffered such injuries, it was almost revulsion, or even…hatred?

Impossible. He must be more exhausted than he'd thought if he could imagine such a thing. Twins were closer than almost any other people, and in their case, with Sara putting herself through pregnancy on her sister's behalf, they were bound to be closer than most.

Then, without a single question about how Sara came to be so injured, Zara held out a hand towards him in a blatantly theatrical plea.

'Oh, Danny, I'm so sorry for putting you through this but…' She bit her lip and peered up at him. 'I just couldn't cope with it any more. It was all just too much.'

'Couldn't bear what?' he asked, not buying her pantomime for a minute, although there must be something serious behind her actions. Someone as self-centred as Zara didn't do anything without planning it down to the last step, like her plan to seduce him.

'Well, didn't you read my note?' she demanded crossly. She was clearly wrong-footed by the fact that he didn't know what she was talking about, but he had no doubt he would be hearing all about it in exhaustive detail.

'I didn't see any note. When did you write it? Where did you put it?' he demanded. It certainly hadn't been on the mantelpiece when he'd put the picture of the scan there, although he hadn't really been looking at anything other than those two indeterminate dark blobs with the bright flashes where their hearts were beating.

'Oh, Danny,' she cried, and accepted the pretty handkerchief her mother offered, actually managing to squeeze out a tear or two. 'I poured my heart out to you…told you how insecure I was feeling…how afraid that… Oh, what's the use?' she said petulantly, and turned her back on him.

'She's overwrought,' Audrey said in a stage whisper. 'She'll feel better when she's had a good night's sleep in her own bed.' She turned her attention to Mr Shah. 'When can we take her home? Do we have to fill in any papers?'

'Oh, my dear Mrs…Mrs Walker,' he said after a quick glance at Zara's notes to refresh his memory. 'Your daughter is perfectly within her rights to sign her self out of hospital, but I certainly wouldn't advise it.'

'Why on earth not?' challenged Frank. 'We've all been waiting for her to wake up and now she has. Surely that's an end to the whole miserable episode.'

'I wish it were, sir, believe me,' the consultant said with a shake of his head. 'Unfortunately, the fact that your daughter has woken doesn't mean that all the drugs have left her body, and until the drip has neutralised the para-cetamol, the drug could still be doing damage to her liver.'

'But…' Audrey looked almost comically disappointed.

'It really would be better if she stayed until we can give her a clean bill of health. She probably still feels rather shaky and tired and would rather not make a journey before she's absolutely ready.'

Dan smothered a grin when he recognised the way the ICU consultant had got the measure of the Walker family. To suggest, obliquely, that Zara needed specialist attention for a little longer was the one strategy that her parents wouldn't want to argue with.

After that, it wasn't very long before the senior sister had used a similar technique for persuading Audrey and Frank that it would be in everybody's best interests if they went home and had a good night's sleep.

Sleep! It had been so long since he'd done it that he felt quite punch-drunk, but something still wouldn't let him leave until he'd gone to check that Sara was finally getting some rest. After Zara's little pout he'd turned to say some-thing to her, but neither the wheelchair nor its occupant had been anywhere in sight.

'What do you think you're doing?' he growled when he found her clothed in a set of baggy blue scrubs and trying to work out how she could use a pair of crutches with one shoulder taped up after a dislocation. 'Are you completely crazy? You should be in bed, allowing your injuries to start healing.'

'And that's exactly where I'll be as soon as I get home,' she countered with a stubborn lift of her chin.

'And exactly how were you intending getting there?' he asked, wondering what it would do to his credibility as a doctor if he stood in the middle of the corridor and screamed out his frustration. Why wouldn't the wretched woman see that he was trying to take care of her?

'Well, as walking is plainly out of the question until I'm a little more proficient, I would have thought that the obvious alternative is a taxi,' she snapped in frustration, standing on one leg and clearly in danger of losing her balance and falling over as she tried to put her coat on.

'And when you get home?' he persisted. 'How were you going to get up all those stairs to your little eyrie?'

He almost felt sorry when he saw her shoulders slump in defeat.

'I can't stay in here, Dan,' she said turning those golden hazel eyes on him in mute appeal. 'Won't you help me?'

'If you're really adamant about leaving, you've got two choices. Either I can drop you off at you parents' house—'

'No way!' she exclaimed with a shudder. 'I haven't spent a night there since I left for medical school and I don't intend changing that. What's the other alternative?'

'That I take you home to my flat.'

'*Your* flat?'

Her expression was so shocked that he hurried to continue. 'I—*we*—do have a spare room, Sara, and I'm sure that your sister would be delighted to know you're somewhere safe.'

Under her breath she muttered something that sounded very much like, 'I doubt it.' He almost asked her to explain but as she was conceding defeat over donning her coat it looked as if he'd at least won that round, even if was only to get her to stay here for the few hours left till morning.

'I'll give you a lift after morning rounds if the orthopod gives you the all-clear, and see what we can do to make you comfortable and safe...all three of you,' he added quickly when she bristled again at the suggestion that she couldn't take care of herself. He wasn't above using her pregnancy as a weapon if it got her to take care of herself. 'The last thing you need is to have a fall down the stairs. You might not be so lucky a second time.'

CHAPTER FIVE

SARA felt as if she'd been tricked into staying in hospital for the last few hours.

It had taken her some time to recognise the way Dan had played on her concern for the two tiny beings residing inside her to persuade her to agree, and she'd even had to smile at his astuteness, but she had no intention of staying any longer. Now was the perfect time to make good her escape, while the staff were all too busy elsewhere to notice her going. What did it matter that she would now be leaving in daylight in a pair of oversized scrubs that looked like a clown's baggy pyjamas and a coat that looked as if someone had rolled in the gutter in it—which she had.

'Maybe the dry-cleaners will be able to do something with it,' she muttered as she awkwardly balanced her borrowed crutches across the arms of the wheelchair to reach for the button to call for the lift. If the coat wasn't salvageable…well, it was easy come, easy go. It had been one of the items Zara had been throwing out because she'd needed to make room for more up-to-the-minute items, ir-respective of the fact that it was made of some horrendously expensive fabric like cashmere or vicuna. All Sara knew was that it was the most deliciously warm coat she'd ever worn and she'd be loath to lose it. She certainly wouldn't be able to replace it with anything as good.

'Making your escape?' said a deep voice behind her, and she jumped so high she had to scrabble to hold onto the crutches.

'Dan! Don't do that!' she snapped as her heart gave its familiar leap in response to his closeness.

'I had a feeling you wouldn't be waiting about this morning,' he said wryly. 'It's nice to be proved right.'

'Actually, I was just going to call in to ICU to see what Zara's latest results are. Have you already been? Do you know?'

The lift gave a quiet ding and the doors slid open to disgorge half a dozen assorted staff and visitors. 'Let's find out together,' he suggested as he took charge and wheeled her into the lift. Then the doors slid closed and the two of them were trapped in the enclosed space, isolated and alone in a way she'd been careful to avoid ever since the day Zara had turned up to be introduced to her tall, dark and handsome doctor friend.

'Sara, are you really well enough to be leaving so soon?' he asked quietly, and her heart gave a stupid extra beat when she saw the caring expression in his eyes.

He's a doctor. Caring's what he does, she reminded herself firmly, just in case she got the idea that it was her as a person that he cared about.

'I'll cope,' she said firmly. 'I'm a fit, healthy person, so I'll soon be on the mend. You don't have to worry about me.'

Her timing was perfect as the doors slid open just as she finished speaking, and the people waiting to board the lift prevented Dan from saying anything more.

'Ah, Daniel. Good. I'm glad you're here,' Mr Shah said, almost as soon as they'd set foot in the unit.

'Problems?' Sara heard the edge in his voice that told her he'd been expecting this conversation.

'More problems than I'd like,' the consultant admitted as he showed them into his office. 'Your wife's liver enzymes are raised and rising but time is critical. If only we knew exactly how long it was since she took the overdose. We'd have some idea how much further they might go.'

Sara felt sick as she took in the information. She knew that the raised enzyme levels were evidence of liver damage but she also knew that the number of hours between overdose and the start of treatment was very important. If a patient received the antidote within eight hours there was a far better chance of saving the liver from permanent, if not fatal, damage.

In her mind's eye she replayed the split second before she'd been struck by that car, the instant when she'd been looking straight towards whoever was driving it and had seen her own face looking back at her.

Had it been her own face, reflected back at her from the windscreen, or had the person behind the wheel been the only other person in the world with a face exactly like hers?

She didn't want to know, couldn't bear to know if it had been Zara, because whoever it had been, there was absolutely no doubt in her mind that they had aimed the car at her deliberately, that they had intended to kill her and the babies inside her.

But…logic told her that knowing might be essential for Zara's health. If she *had* been the driver, that would mean that she probably hadn't taken the paracetamol until she'd returned home. That would give Mr Shah the timeline he needed to gauge how much more aggressive his treatment needed to be if he was to be able to rescue Zara's liver.

She was still conducting her silent debate when one of the nurses ushered her parents into the office to join them.

'I'm afraid Zara won't be going home today,' the consultant stated firmly as soon as the pleasantries were over.

'But I've got everything ready for—' Audrey protested.

'She's not well enough to leave today,' he said. 'Her latest results are showing us a problem with her liver and she needs to stay here until we know she's stable.'

'Her liver? What's wrong with her liver?' Frank demanded with a look of disbelief. 'She's never been a big drinker, not like some of these girls who go out and get drunk all the time.'

'Partly she's having the problem because she's underweight,' Mr Shah explained patiently. 'Her liver didn't have enough reserves, so when her body started to break down the paracetamol, it began damaging the tissues of the liver.'

'So, how bad is it?' Frank was suddenly very subdued, as though the severity of the situation was only now coming home to him. 'And is it going to get any worse?'

'The damage means that her liver will develop areas of

necrosis—that means the tissue dies,' he explained hastily when he saw their puzzled expressions. 'We don't know yet whether it's going to get any worse. It's just a case of wait and see.'

'How long will we have to wait? Weeks? Months?' Audrey asked tearfully, clutching her husband's hand like a lifeline.

'Not as long as that. Usually, it's no more than a few days before we can tell whether the liver is damaged beyond repair.'

'What happens then?' Audrey was pale and shaky but clearly intent on fighting for her precious daughter. 'What are you going to do to make her well again? Will she need medication or dialysis or what?'

'Dialysis isn't an option—it can only be used for kidney failure—but some patients with quite severe liver damage can recover with the right diet and support. For the rest, there are surgical options, but we won't go into that unless it becomes necessary.'

The meeting broke up then, with her parents hurrying off to spend time with Zara while Sara was left trying to manoeuvre wheelchair and crutches out of the office without taking a chunk out of the door.

'Let me,' Dan said, and took over the propulsion again. And even though being this close to him caused every nerve in her body to tense up, she wasn't about to refuse the loan of some muscle power to get her to the lift.

'Thank you,' she murmured, careful not to look in his direction while they waited for the lift to arrive. She was grateful they weren't the only ones in it this time—the more people sharing the space the better if she wasn't to risk making a complete fool of herself. How long would it take before he realised that she'd never got over him, even though he'd abandoned her in favour of marrying her sister?

She could have groaned when he insisted on pushing her across the expanse of the main reception hall and out of the electronically controlled doors.

'Where do you want to go?' he asked, absent-mindedly flicking the keys in his hand against his leg.

'I can get a taxi,' she pointed out with a glance towards the couple already waiting outside the front of the hospital, their drivers chatting to each other with the ease of long acquaintance.

'Ah, but will it be driven by someone willing to stay long enough to make sure you get up your stairs safely? Are you willing to risk falling down and breaking something else—or injuring the babies?'

He didn't play fair, Sara grumbled silently as she tried to make herself comfortable on the plush grey upholstery. If he hadn't mentioned the babies, she would have stuck to her guns, she told herself as she tried to get her cast into the footwell, grateful that he'd thought to slide the passenger seat back as far as possible to accommodate her lack of mobility.

She breathed a sigh of relief when she was finally able to click the seat belt into position then regretted it when she drew in that tantalising mixture of soap and man that would forever signify Dan.

Think of something to talk about, she told herself sternly as he pulled out of the car park, but the only topic that came to mind was Zara. Still, it did prompt an idea.

'Nice car,' she commented blandly. 'What sort is Zara driving these days?'

'I didn't think you were into cars.' There was a hint of laughter in his voice, the laughter that she'd loved to share with him when she'd believed they'd had a future together. 'You don't even own one, do you?'

'I didn't see the point of buying one for the sake of it,' she said stiffly, fighting off the memories. 'I live within walking distance of the hospital and the shops, and if I need to go further afield, there's always a taxi or the train.'

'So, why the interest in Zara's vehicle?'

'Just wondering if you ever let her drive yours.' That was bound to get her the information she wanted. She knew how much he loved his bad-boy black BMW with its pale grey interior, had been with him the day he'd taken delivery of it, the first new car he'd ever owned.

'No way!' he exclaimed fervently. 'But she insisted that she needed to be able to get about and wanted something equally sporty, so…'

'His and hers? Matching cars?' she teased and held her breath.

'Well, yes,' he admitted uncomfortably, then added, 'Except hers is metallic silver with black upholstery.'

'Big difference!' she teased again, although how she found the words she didn't know. A silver car with dark upholstery. That was an image that would be imprinted in her memory for the rest of her life.

But there must be thousands of silver BMWs. It could

have been any one of them, said the corner of her brain that didn't want to believe that her sister could have done that to her. Except, she argued with herself as her fingers crept up to trace the scar on her forehead, you know what she was capable of when she was just a little girl. She's grown up now, but has she grown out of such tendencies or has the scale of them grown with her?

'I hope you won't mind if I stop off at my flat first,' he said, and she was so relieved that he was interrupting the darkening spiral of her thoughts that she would have agreed to almost anything. 'It shouldn't take me long, but you can come up and wait for me if you like.'

'And have to go through all that effort of posting myself back into the car? No, thank you,' she said. 'If you park in the underground car park, I'll be quite safe while I wait for you.'

He tried to change her mind but she was adamant, a new plan already fully formed in her head.

As soon as he disappeared from view she opened the passenger door and began the time-consuming struggle to extricate herself from the car. All the while her pulse was racing, afraid that she wouldn't have time to achieve what she wanted to before he came back.

'A silver BMW with a black interior,' she muttered aloud, having had to admit defeat with the crutches when her recently dislocated shoulder refused to take the pressure. Anyway the pain was too great and she didn't dare to do it any more damage or it could be a problem for the rest of her life.

So it was her eyes rather than her feet that set off along

the row of cars while she leant against Dan's, her eyebrows lifting a little more with each expensive model she recognised, but in spite of the fact that there were two other BMWs, neither was silver with a black interior.

'So much for my idea of seeing whether there was any damage on her car,' she grumbled as she made her halting way back to Dan's vehicle. But if it wasn't here, where could it be? Zara certainly hadn't driven herself to the hospital in it.

'Sara, what's the matter? Why did you get out of the car?' She hadn't even heard the lift coming down but there was Dan hurrying towards her across the oil-stained concrete.

'Um…I had a touch of cramp and needed to get out to move about a bit,' she invented clumsily, hating not to tell the truth, but how could she make such an accusation without a single shred of proof?

'Are you ready to get back in or would you rather change your mind?' he offered. 'It wouldn't take me five minutes to put clean sheets on the bed.'

Dan and bed in the same sentence weren't the ideal combination to ensure she had a good sleep. 'I'd rather go where I'm surrounded by my own things,' she said, while her brain was trying to find a way to get the answers she needed.

Finally, there was only one way.

'I couldn't see Zara's car in the garage,' she said, hoping it sounded like idle conversation while he steered them out of the garage and back onto the street.

'You wouldn't. It's usually parked in the slot next to

mine, but apparently she had an argument with a bollard the other day and dropped it off at the garage to have some scratches repaired…not for the first time, I might tell you,' he added with a chuckle.

'So, when did she take it to the garage?' Sara asked, and the frowning glance he threw her way told her that she'd pushed too far.

'Sara, what's all this about?' he asked as he drew up in front of the converted Victorian house she lived in. He turned to face her. 'Why so many questions about Zara's car? What do you *really* want to know?'

Sara swallowed hard when she met his gaze, knowing the frightening level of intelligence contained behind those green eyes. There would be no point insulting that intelligence with a half-baked invention.

'I wanted to know because…' She swallowed again, afraid that this was going to be the moment when she lost all semblance of friendship with the man she'd never stopped loving. 'Because the car that ran me down was a silver BMW with dark-coloured upholstery and I'm almost certain that it was driven by a woman with long blonde hair.'

To say he looked shocked by the implied accusation was an understatement, and the longer she looked at those eyes and the way they widened and darkened endlessly with the repercussions had her hurrying into speech again.

'I can't believe that *anyone* would want to do such a thing deliberately, least of all Zara, but…but I needed to know…about her car, and about the damage she did to it. Then I'll have the proof that it *wasn't* my sister who tried to…to…' She choked on the press of tears and couldn't say another word but, then, she'd already said more than enough if his expression was anything to go by.

There was an agonisingly long silence in the car while she tried to concentrate on keeping the tears back. Crying was one of Zara's favourite weapons and all her life Sara had consciously fought against them for just that reason.

'Well, then, there's only one thing to do, isn't there?' Dan said suddenly as he released his seat belt. His voice was so frighteningly devoid of any emotion that Sara felt sick.

'W-what?' she stammered as he threw his door open and prepared to slide out. 'What *are* you going to do, Dan?'

He didn't answer until he reached her side of the car and pulled the passenger door wide. 'Find some answers, of course,' he said briskly. 'Now, leave your crutches in the car because they're no use to you till your shoulder's a good deal less painful, and let me give you a hand out of there. You need to get some proper clothes on if you want to travel in my car again.'

Her startled grin must have been the reason he'd added that last proviso, and it had worked. In fact, it had worked so well that she didn't even think of objecting when he virtually carried her up the four flights of stairs that led to her little flat up under the eaves.

'Hop to it,' he joked as she did just that with one hand against the wall on her way to her minuscule bedroom. 'Give me a shout if you need any help.'

'As if,' she growled as she unwrapped herself from the grubby coat and shed the hospital scrubs in short order.

Clothing for her upper half wasn't a problem, barring the twinges from multiple bruises and pulling scabs while she put them on. All she had to remember was to put her injured arm in first because the strapping didn't allow for very much mobility.

Unfortunately, her underwear didn't come with a tie waist and the cast wouldn't fit through the appropriate hole when she did manage to get her foot through it and pull it up with her other toes, even though it was a pair designed for halfway-through-pregnancy mums.

'Damn, damn, damn,' she muttered as she pushed the stretchy fabric off with the other foot and heaved herself up off the end of the bed for another trawl through her underwear drawer.

'Sara, I'm not being funny but... You must be very stiff and sore this morning and I can imagine that it's almost impossible to manoeuvre things over that cast,' Dan said at the very moment that she unearthed the black lacy thong that she'd bought to cheer herself up shortly after Zara had made that fateful visit to A and E. It was testament to how well it had worked that it still sported a dangling price tag.

Well, she thought with a fatalistic shrug as she tugged the tag off and flicked it towards the bin in the corner, it was probably the only underwear she possessed that would work. As for outer clothes, the only ones to hand that were wide enough to encompass the cast without having to resort to splitting a seam was a pair of heavy silk loose-fitting palazzo pants with a drawstring waist, not unlike the scrubs she'd just taken off, now that she came to think about it.

'I could keep my eyes closed and take directions if you need a hand,' he offered, and the suggestion was so sensible, so helpful, so considerate, so *Daniel* that she felt the threat of tears again. And he wouldn't even have to see her bruises, scabs and bulges if he kept his eyes shut.

'You promise to keep your eyes shut?' she demanded as a strange thrill of excitement shot through her that he would offer to do such an intimate thing for her.

'I promise,' he said firmly. 'Now, is it safe to come in?'

'No! Wait!' she shrieked as she saw the door start to swing open, and grabbed for the nearest thing to cover her naked lower half. 'Now it's safe,' she announced, all too conscious of the slight quiver in her voice and hoping like mad that Dan couldn't hear it.

'So, what do you want me to do?' he offered, and suddenly a whole X-rated scenario leapt into her head and she could feel the heat of a deep crimson blush move up her throat and over her face. 'Which bit do you want to do first and how do you want to play it?'

Her imagination leapt into overdrive and it was only the patient expression on his face and the interrogative eyebrow sending creases over his forehead that reminded her he was waiting for an answer.

'Um, if I put my...my underwear on the floor and step into it, could you pull it up for me—just as far as my knees?' she added hastily, and was treated to one of Dan's most devastating grins.

'Spoilsport!' he complained with a long-suffering air. 'OK, where is this...underwear?' She knew his hesitation was a deliberate copy of her own but was determined to ignore it. It was enough that she had to sort out which way the thong needed to be placed on the floor without having to cope with the soft wolf-whistle Dan gave when he caught sight of them.

'Well, well, well!' he murmured as he bent to position the scrap of fabric at her feet. 'Who would have thought it?'

'And why shouldn't I wear something pretty?' she demanded, stung by his reaction.

'These aren't just pretty,' he said, his voice sounding strangely husky as he began to slide them up past her ankles and on towards her knees, every inch a sensual torment as her eyes followed them all the way. 'Pretty is lace and flowers and pink and white. *This* scrap of noth-ingness is something else entirely!'

'That's far enough,' she said hurriedly, embarrassed all over again when her voice ended on a squeak. 'I can manage from there,' she assured him, and he gave another sigh and shook his head.

'What's next, then?' he asked, nearly catching her settling the slender elastic straps over her hips.

'Those trousers, please.' She pointed at the silky pile on the corner of the bed. 'You might need to feed them up my legs a little way before I can stand up without treading on the bottoms of them.'

'Hey,' he said brightly as he got the job right the first time. 'I've just realised that this is good practice for when I'm helping those children in there to learn how to dress.'

And that was just the reminder she'd needed, she told herself when she was sitting in his car a few minutes later.

It had been absolute agony to try to keep some distance between them on the way down the stairs when she had needed his help every step of the way, but that was what she'd *had* to do. It had been so wonderful to slip into the light-hearted banter that had been so much a part of their relationship, even in those early days, but that was all in the past.

She couldn't believe what the two of them had been doing up in her room. They'd almost been flirting with each other and there was no excuse for that. Dan was a married man and he was married to her sister. To allow anything to happen between them would be the worst sort of betrayal and she just couldn't be a part of it.

The trouble was, her love for him hadn't died when he'd married Zara, no matter how much she'd prayed that it would. Yes, he was the father of the babies she carried and, yes, she would love nothing better than that he would be at her side as together they guided them through childhood and into adulthood, but it wasn't going to happen.

'Because he's married,' she whispered fiercely as he circled the front of the car. 'He's married to your sister and the only thing he wants of you is what you're carrying in your womb—the babies that Zara can't give him.'

Something in her expression must have told him that her mood had changed because the atmosphere in the car that could have been too cosy and intimate was all business as he put the key into the ignition.

'So, what *do* you remember of your accident?' he asked as he joined the stream of traffic heading back into town.

Too much, was the first thought that came into her head,

but she knew he needed a logical answer from her. She was just overwhelmingly grateful that he hadn't angrily brushed her suggestion off as the ravings of someone who'd had an unfortunate random accident. He could have accused her of using the incident to get some sort of petty revenge against Zara or…

'Sara?' She'd almost forgotten he was waiting for an answer, so lost had she become in her thoughts.

'I always walk home the same way…out of the back of the hospital and past that little parade of shops, just in case I need to pick anything up on the way.' She glanced across briefly and saw the tiny frown pulling his dark brows together, the way they always did when he was concentrating. Afraid she'd lose her train of thought if she looked any longer, she stared straight ahead and continued.

'I'd gone over the crossroads and was just crossing one of those little turnings that seem to lead round to the back of the shops, for deliveries or something…not a real residential road, if you know what I mean?'

Out of the corner of her eye she saw his brief nod but he didn't say a word to distract her—she could manage to distract herself without any help.

'I heard a car coming and glanced towards it and I remember thinking that it wasn't the sort of vehicle I expected to see coming out of there, then I realised that it didn't seem to be slowing down and I realised that I was too far away from the kerb to get to safety and when I tried to turn away so that the impact wouldn't hurt the baby, my foot slipped on the wet cobbles and then the car hit me and I went down and my head hit the kerb and…and I woke up in A and E.'

'So, what made you think it might have been Zara?' he asked, his white knuckles clenched around the steering-wheel testament to the fact that he wasn't nearly as calm as he sounded. 'It sounds as if it all happened pretty quickly…too quickly to have seen anything much.'

Sara knew he was right, but she also knew what she'd seen. 'Well, I can now tell you from firsthand experience that when it looks as if you're going to die, there is a split second that's imprinted indelibly in your mind. It's so clear that if I were any sort of an artist, I'd be able to draw it for you with the accuracy of a photograph.'

'Tell me,' he prompted softly. 'What do you see in the photo in your mind?'

'The cobbles are wet and shiny, and there's a skinny cat running towards the shadows of a pile of cardboard boxes and his fur's all wet from the rain, and the light is gleaming off the car as it comes towards me…off the paintwork and the chrome and the windscreen as it's getting closer… And when I realised that it was going to hit me, I realised that it might hurt the baby…this was before I knew there were two of them,' she interjected in a crazy non sequitur. 'But when I put my hand over my bump—as if that would protect it from half a ton of car—the person in the car pressed their foot down on the accelerator and I heard the engine roar in response.'

Dan muttered something under his breath but the scene inside her head and the emotions she'd been feeling at the time were so strong that she paid him no heed.

'I was staring at it in disbelief, so sure that the person would put the brakes on, but she was staring straight ahead—straight at me—and her hair was long and blonde and down over her shoulders and her face… At first I thought it was *my* face reflected back at me and that could *still* be what I saw but…' She drew in a shaky breath and continued, 'Her hands were gripped round the steering-wheel…up at the top of the wheel so that her thumbs were nearly touching…and I have the impression that her nails were really long and painted with a dark varnish, but I can't be sure what colour…' She closed her eyes for a moment in the hope that it would help her to focus, but it didn't get any clearer so she went back to her narrative, to the part that still made her feel guilty that it had happened at all.

'Dan, I really did try to get out of its path,' she assured him fervently, desperate that he should believe that she'd done her best to protect his child, 'but it was coming at me far too fast and then my foot slipped but the car still hit my leg and I spun round… Actually at the time I thought it was the streetlight that was spinning round me…but I was falling and falling and I couldn't stop myself and then my head hit the ground and everything went black.'

He was silent for so long that she wondered if he was ever going to speak to her again. What was he thinking? That she was crazy? That he'd made a monumental mistake in asking her to carry his children in case she passed her craziness on to his innocent offspring?

'So, what part of the car would have hit you?' he asked, his voice sounding more like a rough growl until he cleared his throat, and tears threatened when she realised that his question meant he hadn't dismissed what she'd told him out of hand. 'Would it have been the front, the wing or both?'

CHAPTER SIX

DAN and Sara stared down at the broken light on the passenger side of the BMW while the mechanic wiped his hands on a rag so black and oily that it couldn't possibly be doing any good.

'It's not the first time she's brought it in but, then, that's women drivers for you,' he added with blatant chauvinism and a knowing wink for Dan.

Sara didn't have the breath to argue this slur on her half of mankind. She was still devastated by the evident damage to her sister's car.

'You say she's brought it in for repairs before?' Dan questioned, and from the tone of his voice that fact was news to him.

'Oops! Sorry if I'm dumping you in it, love,' he said to Sara, 'but last time it was the back bumper. She said she'd managed to reverse it into a bollard somewhere up near the London Eye.'

'And what did she tell you about this?' Dan pointed to the recent damage.

His uncomfortable look in her direction, not quite

meeting her eye, made Sara suddenly realise that he thought *she* was Zara, being taken to task by a far-too-calm husband. He probably thought her rapidly developing black eye and the dressing on her forehead were signs of wife abuse, she realized with a crazy urge to laugh.

'Actually, she didn't say anything because she didn't drop it off until after the garage closed. And last night, that was six o'clock because we were waiting for a customer to come and pick his vehicle up and settle his bill—you don't mind staying open a bit longer when it's for a good customer bringing you money, do you?'

His attempt at comradeship fell flat as Dan leant forward to take a closer look at the damaged light, reaching out to fiddle with the shattered remains for a second before he straightened up again.

'Well, thank you for your time,' he said politely. 'Let me know when the vehicle's ready for collection, won't you?' He wrapped a supportive arm around Sara's waist and helped her to hop the couple of steps to his car.

'So, it could have been any number of things that caused the damage, if she's in the habit of bumping into things,' Sara said almost before he'd closed his door, trying to find a logical reason why the damage they'd seen had nothing to do with her injuries.

She hated the thought that her sister might have wished her ill, although that long-ago episode with the piece of wood and the 'accident' that hadn't been accidental at all. Still, she was desperately afraid that she'd set something in motion that couldn't be stopped.

But, then, did she want it stopped? If her sister *had* tried to hurt her by driving that car straight at her then it was important to find out why or she might never be safe. And what if it had been the pregnancy that had been Zara's target? Sara couldn't bear the thought that her precious babies might be put at risk if she handed them over to her sister.

Had Zara been taking some of the more exotic designer drugs that her colleagues brought back from their foreign photo shoots? If so, they could have disturbed the balance of her mind and caused her to do such an outrageous thing.

But there hadn't been any evidence of strange chemicals in any of her blood tests—at least, nothing beyond the sleeping tablets and paracetamol that they already knew about.

She shook her head, at a loss to know what to think. It was already aching enough with out this mental stress, but that was probably because she'd been on her feet far too much already today. It certainly wasn't what she would want a patient of hers to do after such an incident.

Into the silence of the car came the unmistakable sound of Dan's pager and he cursed softly under his breath as he tried to find a break in the busy traffic to pull over to the side of the road.

Once there, it only took seconds before he'd used his mobile phone to call the unit and Sara suddenly realised that it was the first time she'd heard him speak since they'd left the garage.

What had he been thinking while her brain had been strangled by conflicting ideas? Had he dismissed her claim that she'd recognised Zara as her assailant now that he'd seen that there was no real evidence or was he, too, worried about the ramifications for the children she was carrying if their mother-to-be had really tried to injure them?

'That was your mother,' he announced as he ended the call and pulled back out into the traffic. 'She says that we need to go back to the hospital straight away. Zara's next set of tests results have come in.'

'Is she worse?' Sara demanded anxiously, because, no matter what she'd done, Zara was her twin and she loved her.

'Your mother didn't say. All she told me was that we had to go straight to the hospital, so…' He shrugged, his eyes never leaving the road as he navigated the quickest route.

'Mum. Dad. What's happened? What's the problem with the latest results?' Sara asked as soon as Dan pushed her into the unit in a hastily purloined wheelchair and found her parents just inside the doors, as though they'd been waiting impatiently for them to arrive.

'What took you so long?' her mother demanded, whirling to hurry up the corridor. 'Mr Shah has got the results in his office and he needs to have a word with us.'

Sara suspected that the consultant was waiting to have a word with Dan rather than her parents. After all, as her husband he was legally Zara's next of kin.

'Daniel, come in, come in,' the dapper gentleman invited, but it was Audrey who pushed in ahead of the wheelchair and took one of the two available chairs, closely followed by her husband. Daniel was left to prop himself up on the wall beside Sara to wait for Mr Shah to open Zara's file sitting on his desk.

'The nurse said you've had some more results, and I want to know when we're going to be able to take our daughter home,' Audrey said with the air of a general firing the opening salvo in a war she fully intended winning.

An expression of annoyance slid briefly across the consultant's face, probably at the knowledge that a nurse had been giving out more information than she should have. Sara could imagine that before the shift was over her superior would be having a sharply worded conversation with whoever was responsible.

In the meantime, the man's face had settled into the sort of bland expression that always preceded less-than-welcome news.

'Unfortunately, the news isn't good enough for us to be able to give you that sort of information,' he said quietly. 'Her liver function tests are giving us more cause for concern and it looks as if there may be more necrosis than we'd expected.'

'Necrosis?' Audrey pounced on the word. 'What's necrosis?'

'It means that sections of her liver have been damaged and are dying, so they are no longer able to perform their proper function.'

'So it's the same as what you found on the last tests,' she summarised for herself.

'Yes and no,' he prevaricated. 'Yes, it's the same condition but, no, it's not the same as before because the condition has worsened.'

'So, what are you going to do about it?' Frank asked, and Sara wasn't surprised to see how pale he was looking at the thought that his precious daughter's health wasn't improving the way they'd hoped.

'I'm afraid we can't do much more than we're already doing as far as infusing the antidote into her system and supporting her and keeping an eye on the concentration of various components in her blood. It's still very much a case of wait and see, but I thought you would want to be informed of the results so that you would know to prepare yourselves in case—'

'Would a transplant cure it?' Audrey interrupted, clearly unwilling to hear that particular eventuality even as a theory.

'Well, yes, we can do liver transplants in some conditions—for example, in people with cirrhosis or hepatitis and also in some cases where the patient has had medication toxic to the liver—but the success rate is not as good as for kidney transplantation and there's still the problem of finding a compatible liver donor while there's still time to do the operation.'

'Well, that's not a problem, then…not for Zara,' her mother announced with a beaming smile. 'Sara will give her one of hers. I've seen it on television and they said that identical twins are a perfect match. Once you operate, Zara will be as good as new.'

'No,' Sara said sharply, and her mother turned on her with a look of utter disbelief on her face.

'What do you mean, *no*? Sara, you *can't* refuse to help your sister if she needs one of yours.'

'Mother, I've only *got* one liver, so I can't give it to her. The operation would mean chopping a chunk of mine away and that's major surgery. Anyway, I doubt if you'd find a surgeon willing to do it because I'm pregnant and it wouldn't be good for the babies.'

'Well, then, you'll have to get rid of the babies,' her mother announced with a breathtaking lack of feeling for the unborn lives nestling inside her. 'You can't refuse to help save your sister's life. She could die.'

'But you would be quite happy for me to murder *my* babies to save *your* baby?' Sara couldn't believe the pain that thought caused, her heart clenching inside her chest as though every drop of blood had been wrung out of it.

Ever since she'd seen those two hearts on the ultrasound screen, beating so valiantly in spite of the recent trauma, it had brought the reality of her pregnancy home to her the way no amount of reading pregnancy books had done. She felt so connected to those tiny beings, so protective, that the thought of deliberately scouring them out of her womb and flushing them away was anathema.

'So.' She lifted her chin and stared her mother right in the eye. 'What if I refuse to do it?'

'You *can't* refuse because they're not *your* babies, they're Zara's, and if she needs them to die so that she can live—'

It was Sara's turn to interrupt and she did so without a qualm.

'They might be babies I'm *carrying* for Zara, but they're growing in *my* body and from *my* eggs…and what's more, it's *my* liver you're talking about and *no one* can have it if I don't want to give it.'

Her mother broke into noisy sobs and no matter what her father said she wouldn't be consoled.

Sara felt dreadful.

She now knew firsthand just how fiercely a mother would defend her child and couldn't really blame her own mother for wanting to do everything she could to give her daughter a chance of being well again.

But she was a mother, too—at least while those two helpless innocents were still inside her—and she was going to fight every bit as hard for their survival.

Poor Mr Shah didn't seem to know what to do for the best. Her parents were clearly beyond listening to anything he said, even though he repeatedly tried to reassure them that Zara's condition hadn't yet reached the point of no return.

While Dan…

Suddenly, Sara realised that the one person with the most to lose in this whole disastrous situation was the only one who hadn't said a single word.

A single glance in his direction was enough to tell her that he'd retreated behind what she'd privately dubbed his 'stone' face. There wasn't a single emotion visible, until she happened to see the way his hands were clenched into tight fists inside his trouser pockets.

As if her mother had sensed that her attention had wandered she turned a tear-ravaged face to her son-in-law. 'Danny, do something,' she pleaded. 'You have to tell Sara to save my precious girl… You must *make* her give Zara a new liver!'

'No,' he said quietly with a reinforcing shake of his head. 'It's not time for that discussion, Audrey. Listen to what Mr Shah's been trying to tell you. Eighty per cent of patients with even severe liver damage eventually recover on their own, so it's just a case of waiting to see if Zara's liver is going to do the same.'

'But the transplant,' she persisted. 'Because they're identical twins it would be a perfect match and—'

'And it might only give her another year of life,' Dan finished brutally, and literally robbed her of the breath to argue any further, her mouth and eyes open like a gasping fish. 'That's the average survival rate for liver transplants at the moment,' he told her with an air of finality.

Sara knew from reading medical journals that some patients had survived considerably longer. It was probably the poor survival rate of liver cancer transplant patients that brought the overall rate down, but it wasn't accurate statistics that she cared about, it was the fact that he had managed to take her completely out of the firing line…for the moment at least.

'Now,' said Mr Shah, looking unusually flustered by the open warfare he'd just had to witness, 'I think it would be best if you were all to go home and have some rest.'

'Oh, but we haven't seen—' Audrey began, but was totally ignored as he continued inexorably, drawing a line in the sand.

'You may come back at visiting time this evening, but no more than two of you may visit at a time. That will ensure that my patient will have what remains of the day to rest and hopefully give her body a chance to start to recover.'

It was beautifully done, Sara acknowledged wryly as they filed silently out of the consultant's office, but it had left all of them in no doubt who was wielding the power in *his* unit.

'Would you like a lift?' Dan offered quietly, when they'd watched her parents scurry out of the unit before he began to push her in the same direction.

'Don't you have to go to work today?' she asked, desperate to spend what time she could with him but knowing it wasn't a sensible idea. 'You don't have time to keep ferrying me about.'

'Actually, I've got all the time in the world, having just been banned from visiting until evening visiting hours,' he contradicted her as he pushed the button for the lift that was just taking the Walkers down to the main reception area.

All Sara hoped was that it would deliver the two of them to the ground floor before it returned for Dan and her. She didn't think she could bear to be shut up in such a small space with her parents, even for the short time it would take to travel a couple of floors. Mr Shah's office had been bad enough with all that animosity flying around.

'Anyway...' Dan continued, breaking into her silent replay of the moment when her mother had glibly talked about aborting the precious pair already making their presence felt under her protective hand, the curve of her belly already noticeably bigger than it would have been for a single baby at the same number of weeks. 'As I'm on compassionate leave until we know what the situation is with Zara, you can just name your destination.'

'You're going to regret that offer when you find out where I need to go,' she warned, suddenly immeasurably grateful that the rest of the day didn't stretch out in front of her like an arid desert.

'Don't tell me!' Dan said with a groan as he pushed the chair into the waiting lift. 'You need to go shopping!'

'All right, I won't tell you…but that doesn't mean that I don't need to go.'

'All right,' he said with an air of long-suffering that caused several smiles on the faces of the people sharing the lift. 'I offered so I'll take you. Just tell me where you need to go and let's get it over with.'

'What is it with men that they don't like shopping? Is it a genetic thing?' Sara mused aloud, drawing a few smiles of her own, then relented. 'It shouldn't take very long because I only need to do some grocery shopping while I've got someone to carry the bags for me,' she added with a grin, then another thought struck her.

She hesitated for a moment, wondering if there was some other way she could achieve what she wanted and feeling the increased warmth in her cheeks that told her she still hadn't grown out of the habit of blushing. 'I'm sorry but I'll also need to do a bit of clothes shopping.'

He groaned as he waited for their companions to exit first then pushed the wheelchair out into the spacious reception area, thronged as ever by a constantly changing stream of visitors going in and out of the hospital. 'My absolute favourite occupation…not!' he complained in tones of disgust. 'If you're anything like your sister, that will take the rest of the day.'

His assumption stung her more than she had a right to feel and loosened the leash on her tongue. 'Apart from the obvious physical resemblance, over which I have *no* control, I am absolutely *nothing* like my sister!' she snapped. 'And furthermore, far from taking the rest of the day, my shopping should take me no more than five minutes because I only need some comfortable underwear that I can pull on over my cast.'

The words almost seemed to echo around the whole reception area—probably right around the whole of the hospital if the gossip grapevine was operating in its usual mysterious way.

'Oh, good grief!' she moaned, and covered her face when she saw just how many inquisitive faces were turned in their direction, *and* how many of them were sporting broad grins. 'Just get me out of here,' she ordered through clenched teeth, hoping that her long curtain of her hair was hiding the furious heat of her blush.

Dan didn't make the situation any better when he leaned forward and murmured in her ear, '*Comfortable* underwear, Sara? Is that what they call black lace thongs these days?'

'Shut up!' she hissed. 'Just shut up and get me to the car.'

'Ah…in just a second,' he promised as he veered the chair towards the policeman who had just entered the reception area. Then he abandoned her in the middle of the floor to hail the man and the two of them stood talking earnestly for several minutes.

Sara was puzzled when Dan reached into his pocket to pull out a disposable glove, especially when the two of them peered at something inside the glove.

They both had serious expressions on their faces but she was far too far away to hear a single word either of them said, especially with the constant hubbub of passing humanity around her.

'Right! To the car!' Dan announced as he came back to her with the air of a man pleased with a mission accomplished. 'Which would you rather do first—groceries or underwear?' he demanded cheerfully, and the chance to ask what that little episode had been about was lost in the return of her embarrassment.

The grocery shopping was done and they were standing in front of an embarrassing display of female underwear in her favourite high-street shop when Dan's mobile burst into the opening bars of the 1812 Overture.

Grateful for the fact that he wouldn't be looking over her shoulder for a moment, Sara grabbed a packet containing some very definitely non-sexy underwear in a size several larger than her usual one, in the hope that the leg opening would be loose enough to accommodate her cast. But she couldn't resist grabbing another containing a rainbow mix of coloured thongs, telling herself that at least she knew that they were relatively easy to get on. The fact that they were far sexier than the 'old lady' pants in her other hand had absolutely nothing to do with her choice.

There was a frown on his face when he turned back to her.

'That was the hospital,' he began, and her heart leapt into her throat.

'Zara?' she said, immediately feeling guilty that she and Dan were out shopping for her underwear when he should have been waiting for news of his wife. 'Is she worse?'

'No, Sara, no,' he soothed, looking contrite that he hadn't realised that she'd immediately panic. 'It was nothing to do with your sister. It was A and E, asking if I could possibly go in. With the two of us out and two others called in sick—that flu bug that's going around has finally felled Derek when he was only boasting the other day that he never catches anything—they're desperate for another doctor.'

'Desperate? As in…they're building up a logjam of patients and the waiting time's becoming unacceptable?' she asked as she handed over the two packages and had to submit to the indignity of having Dan pay for her underwear, too. He'd already paid for her groceries when she'd belatedly realised that sneaking out of the ward meant that she hadn't collected the purse that had been given into Sister's safekeeping.

'That, and the fact that the traffic lights are on the blink at one of the crossroads and there's been a whole series of prangs as people take the law into their own hands. Pedestrians, cyclists and car-drivers, some more serious than others.'

'Ouch!' She pursed her lips as frustration swept through her. She was certain she would be able to work if she'd only injured her leg. Having a doctor working away in minors, doing the bread-and-butter jobs of stitching and re-trieving foreign bodies from various apertures, wouldn't be too taxing as she would probably be able to sit down for much of it, and it would definitely take some of the load off the rest of them. But with her shoulder strapped to prevent her using anywhere near the full range of motion and with the rest of her body complaining whenever she moved a bruised portion, she'd be more of a liability than a help.

'Stop brooding,' he chided as he pushed her back towards his car at a far faster rate than the companionable stroll with which they'd started their outing. 'You're in no fit state to work, so don't even think about it.'

'Hmm! I see you've added mind-reading to your diagnostic skills,' she sniped, uncomfortable that he'd been able to tell what she was thinking. She hadn't realised that she was so transparent and now worried just how many of her other thoughts he'd been privy to. 'Was that the Masters course in Mind-reading or just the Diploma?'

He laughed. 'Nothing so low-brow. I found I was so good at it that I went all the way to PhD.'

He quickly had her settled in the blissful comfort of the passenger seat and they were on their way—at least, they should have been on their way. The journey from the car park to her flat was only a matter of two streets but they weren't even able to join the stream of traffic on the first one because nothing was moving.

'This isn't going to work,' he said aloud as, with a careful look around, he put the car into a swift U-turn and went back the way they'd come. 'I'm sorry, Sara, but if I'm going to arrive at the hospital in time to do any good I'm going to have to drop you off at our place instead.'

She wanted to object because she really didn't want to spend any time at all in the place that her sister shared with the man *she* loved, but logic told her that she didn't have any other option. Even if she were to ring for a taxi, that would still leave her with the insurmountable obstacle of getting herself and her groceries up four flights of stairs with only one leg and one arm in any sort of usable state.

'I'll come back as soon as the panic's over and deliver you and your goods and chattels as promised,' he assured her as he deposited her shopping bags on the pristine work surface in his kitchen. The journey up in the lift had been a breeze in comparison to the struggle it would have been to install her in her own flat.

'Sling your perishables in the fridge so they don't succumb to the central heating,' he ordered briskly, his mind obviously already racing ahead to what he was going to find when he reached A and E.

'And make yourself at home,' he added, almost as an afterthought, with one hand already reaching out to the front door. 'It shouldn't take more than a couple of hours to sort through the worst of it.' And he was gone.

'Make myself at home?' Sara said into the sudden emptiness of Dan's home and knew it would be impossible.

And it wasn't just because this was the home he shared with Zara. It would have been just as bad *whoever* he was sharing it with because she'd hoped that any home he lived in would have been *her* home, too.

It was because she'd started to dream at one time that it would be her future for the two of them to choose the home they were to share together, to decorate it and choose the furniture and accessories together and… She looked around her, able to see into each of the rooms from her position in this compact central hallway. To the kitchen with the clean-lined Scandinavian cupboards trying desperately to soften the over-abundance of cold stainless-steel appliances and work surfaces; to the bathroom with what should have been a stylish art-deco-inspired combination of black and white that had been made overpowering with the excess of black on floors, walls and paintwork; to the bedroom with the oversized four-poster bed that was totally out of place in such a modern setting and whose voluminous floral drapery looked more like something a pre-schooler would prescribe for a fairy-tale princess.

In fact, the only room in which it looked as if Dan had finally put his foot down was the living room. That alone was an oasis of calm understatement with restful neutral colours a backdrop for the stunning views out of the wide uncluttered windows.

The furniture, when she finally made her way to it, was deliciously comfortable, particularly the reclining chair that was in reach of everything she could need, from the remote control for the television and another one for the stereo system to a wall of bookshelves that had everything from Agatha Christie to massive tomes on emergency radiographic diagnosis.

She quickly realised that this was the one place in the whole flat where she might be able to feel at home, but it wasn't until she turned her head and caught a hint of the shampoo that Dan used that she understood why.

'This is *Dan's* chair,' she said, and cringed as she heard

the words coming back to her sounding like the sort of reverential tones of a besotted fan of her favourite idol.

Disgusted with herself for mooning about like this, she forced herself up onto her feet—well, onto her one weight-bearing foot and her single crutch—and struggled her way into the kitchen.

'It's not your home, so don't go criticising it,' she told herself sternly as she sorted through her shopping to put the perishables away in the enormous American-style fridge. 'And don't go getting comfortable in it either...not even in Dan's chair. You're only going to be here for a short time—just until the panic's over in A and E—and then you'll be back in your own place.'

Her own place with the little poky rooms that were too small to have anything bigger than doll's-house furniture and the old draughty windows and iffy heating.

'But it's mine, everything in it is something I've chosen and it suits me,' she said aloud, even as she silently wondered who she was trying to convince.

It was two hours later that Dan phoned her.

Of course, she didn't know that it was Dan until the an-swering-machine kicked in and she heard his voice pro-jected into the room.

'Sara, pick up the phone...it's Dan,' he announced—as if the sound of his voice wasn't imprinted on every cell in her body.

'Dan?' she said, furious that she sounded so breathless when she'd only had to reach out her hand to pick up the phone. Pathetic!

'Sara, I'm sorry to do this to you, but they really need

me to stay on till the end of the shift. Arne's had to go home with this wretched flu, too. He was nearly out on his feet and we could just about fry eggs on his head.'

Sara chuckled at the mental image painted of her colleague. Arne Kørsvold was an enormous gentle Swedish doctor who disguised the fact that he was rapidly losing his natural platinum-blond hair by shaving his whole head.

'Anyway, if you're OK with it, I'll stay on and work the rest of the shift, then call in for an update on Zara. I promise I'll take you back as soon as I can get away.'

What could she say? A and E's needs were far more urgent than her own so she resigned herself to several more hours of sitting on the chair that faced Dan's recliner and tried not to imagine what it would be like to spend her evenings sharing this lovely room with him.

Sara had no idea when the television programme finally lost her attention and she drifted off to sleep but she was completely out for the count by the time Dan let himself in.

She didn't know how long he stood in the doorway to the living room, watching her sleep; didn't see the way he frowned when he saw the shadows around her eyes that spoke of her exhaustion or the way his eyes softened as they traced the swelling curve of her belly.

The first thing she knew was a hazy realisation that Dan was there and that she was in his arms as he lifted her off the settee. Then he was laying her gently down again and she couldn't help giving a little whimper of disappointment when he took his arms away again.

'Shh,' he whispered softly as he stroked a soothing hand

over her head, and as she drifted off to sleep again, comforted by the fact that he was close to her, she imagined that she felt the butterfly brush of his lips on her forehead.

CHAPTER SEVEN

'I'M GOING to go mad if I have to stay here any longer,' Sara told the four walls of her borrowed bedroom.

She was spending yet another day in Dan's spare room...Dan and *Zara's* spare room, she corrected herself, although it was getting harder and harder to make herself remember that fact.

Because of the continuing staff shortages, Dan had returned to work full time. He was, however, being allowed time to go up at intervals to visit Zara.

Each evening, when he returned to the flat, Dan gave Sara a full report on the latest test results, but Zara's body seemed to be struggling to rid itself of the toxic metabolite of the paracetamol she'd taken.

'No doubt it's because her liver had reduced glutathione stores as the result of her years of drastic dieting,' he said soberly.

'But the liver can regenerate itself,' Sara reminded him. 'Surely the paracetamol hasn't done that much damage that it can't be repaired.' She shook her head and pushed her plate away, unable to eat any more even though it was her favourite tagliatelli carbonara.

'Oh, Dan, I'm in such a muddle. Half of me desperately wants her problem to be the result of taking the drugs earlier in the afternoon, which would mean Zara couldn't possibly be the person driving the car that hit me. But the other half wants just as desperately for it to have been her in the car, because that means the drugs hadn't been in her system so long and she's more likely to recover.'

There was a strange shadow in Dan's eyes but he didn't comment on her dilemma, choosing instead to tell her about one of the department regulars who'd turned up again after an absence of several months showing all the usual signs that she'd fallen off the wagon again.

'Somebody hadn't remembered to flag her name, so the new junior registrar went sailing into the cubicle to find dear old Alice lying there with all her worldly goods piled around her on the bed and snoring her head off.'

'Oh, dear! He didn't touch any of her bags, did he?' Sara chuckled. 'And she woke up and yelled the place down?'

'She started shouting "Fire!" then realised it was a male doctor in the cubicle with her and changed it to "Rape!" with all-too-predictable results.'

'Poor chap!' Sara laughed even louder, remembering her own noisy introduction to Alice and her obsession with her bags. 'I bet he got an even bigger shock when it took less than thirty seconds for the cubicle to fill with half the hospital's security personnel.'

'He was shaking and as white as a sheet and looked as

if he couldn't decide whether he was going into cardiac arrest or giving up his medical career on the spot.'

'The trouble is, rules and regulations are so tight these days about what you can write on a patient's notes, it's difficult to leave a message on them saying, "Treat with extreme caution. Liable to explode," or the hospital legal department would go into orbit. I take it you managed to smooth things over?'

'Well, eventually,' he said, and she was intrigued to see a wash of colour travel over his cheekbones.

'What did she do *this* time?'

'Oh, she was just her usual outrageous self,' he said with a self-conscious shrug.

'You may as well tell me,' she pointed out, her imagination in full flight. 'It will only take a single phone call to find someone else willing to spill the beans, and who knows how much bigger the story has grown in the meantime?'

'Don't remind me,' he groaned. 'I was counting on the fact that you're not fit to work at the moment so that particular bit of gossip would pass you by.'

'So?' she prompted, ignoring the comment about her fitness to work in pursuit of the punchline of the story. Her upcoming return to work was a topic she didn't intend to discuss with him. 'Tell me, tell me. What did she do?'

'It wasn't so much what she did as what she said,' he muttered, looking seriously uncomfortable. 'In front of half the damn department and heaven knows how many patients and relatives she told me she loved my green eyes and invited me into the cubicle to give her a damn good… um…bit of passion.'

Sara burst out laughing. 'Knowing Alice, I bet she didn't use such a genteel phrase.'

Those gorgeous green eyes were sparkling now. 'You'd win that bet,' he conceded. 'The trouble is, I'm never going to hear the end of it.'

'Oh, you will,' she reassured him. 'As soon as the next juicy bit of gossip comes up, that little proposition will all be forgotten…by the rest of your colleagues, at least.'

And it was relaxed conversations like that one last night that were making life so difficult for her. It was becoming harder and harder to stop herself from doing or saying something that would reveal her secret…the fact that she was falling deeper and deeper in love with him the longer she shared his flat.

'Well, enough is enough,' she said firmly as she pushed herself up onto her one good foot and reached for a single crutch.

She'd been practising getting around over the last couple of days. There had been so many empty hours while she'd waited for Dan to return that she'd worked out for herself how she could manoeuvre without needing a pair of them because her shoulder was still too sore to take the weight, even with elbow crutches.

It wasn't an elegant way of getting around, more of a stumbling lop-sided lurch, in fact, and definitely required the presence of a nearby wall as a last resort to stop herself losing her balance completely. The one good thing about it was that she'd almost perfected a way of getting around unaided, and that meant she could leave the danger zone of Dan's spacious flat and take herself back to her own far humbler one.

'It will probably take me a couple of hours to go up all four flights of stairs,' she muttered, feeling exhausted just thinking about it. She stuffed her belongings into a carrier bag, resolutely ignoring the fact that the packet of granny knickers hadn't even been opened, tied the handles to her crutch, then phoned for a taxi. By the time it arrived, she was waiting in the entrance with just a short hop across the pavement left to do.

'Hang on a minute, love,' called the cabbie and heaved his considerable bulk out of the driving seat to give her a steadying hand to climb inside. 'You're in a right mess, aren't you?' he commented soothingly, his eyes meeting hers in the rear-view mirror once he was back in his seat. 'Finally decided to get away from him before he does any worse? You've made the right decision, love. I've got no time for men who think it's OK to knock women about. Need someone to give them a bit of their own medicine.'

'Oh, good grief, no!' Sara laughed. 'It was a car that did this. I nearly got run over the other night.'

'That's right, dear. Get a good story ready to tell people so they won't twig what's really going on. Most of them will probably believe you, but me?' he shook his head and drew in a breath through his teeth. 'I've seen too much of the rough end of life and I can tell the difference, but don't you worry—even if he gets the police out looking for you, I'll never tell where I take you.'

He straightened up in his seat and put the engine into gear. 'Right, now, where do you want to go? To one of the refuges?'

'That's very kind of you, and I'm so glad that there are

people like you who will help battered women, but I've been staying with my sister and brother-in-law—' she didn't see the harm in stretching the truth a little, just to put the man's mind at ease '—ever since I came out of hospital. If you could drop me off at my flat, that will be great.' She gave him the address and was certain that he was quite disappointed he wasn't going to be a brave knight coming to the aid of a maiden in distress.

Except when he drew up outside the multi-storey Victorian building, all his protective instincts seemed to resurrect themselves.

'I hope you're on the ground floor, love,' he said as he lent her a hand again.

'I wish!' she joked, and looked right up towards the very top windows. 'That's me, all the way up there.' And then, no matter how much she tried to reassure him that she could manage, he insisted on keeping her company all the way up all four flights, carrying her bag of belongings in case they unbalanced her and steadying her when her poor overworked leg began to tremble with overuse.

Sara was close to collapse when she finally got the key in the lock and swung the door wide, screwing her nose up at the shut-in smell that seemed to gather even in the space of a couple of days. Then she had a battle to make the man accept the proper fare for bringing her home, and when she tried to add a tip to thank him for spending the time to help her all the way up the stairs he drew himself up with an air of injured dignity.

'I didn't do that for money, love. I did that because you were someone who needed a helping hand. Now, you take this.' He handed her a business card. 'If you need to go anywhere, you ring that number and ask them to send George.'

'Oh, that's just perfect,' she said with a little quiver. 'Just like St George killing the dragon, you came to the aid of a lady in distress.'

He snorted and went a bit pink. 'I don't reckon my missus thinks I'm any sort of saint, but I know what you mean. Now, you take care of yourself.'

He was just about to shut her front door behind him when she remembered what she'd planned to do that evening.

'Oh, George,' she called. 'You don't go off work before seven, do you? Only I'll be needing a taxi to get to the hospital for visiting hours.'

'I told you, love, you need me, I'll be here,' he said with a broad grin. 'Will a quarter to seven be early enough for you?'

'Perfect. I'll see you then.'

It was just after seven o'clock when the lift chimed to announce its arrival on Zara's floor.

This time, thank goodness, she wasn't trying to get about with her single crutch because as soon as she'd arrived in A and E, courtesy of George, she'd been whisked off by a bevy of colleagues and given the loan of a wheel-chair.

'At least my immediate welcome in the department seemed to put his mind at rest,' she mused as she wheeled her awkward one-handed way towards Zara's room, then an alternative suddenly struck her. 'Or perhaps he took it as proof that they know me well because I'm always in here for treatment.'

She was still smiling at that thought when she tapped on Zara's door and began to push it open.

'There she is!' Zara announced, her face twisting into an unattractive scowl. 'And look at that smirk on her face. She just couldn't wait to get her foot in the door, could she? All this time she's resented the fact that Danny chose me and she waited until I'm too ill to do anything about it to move in with him and—'

'Zara!' Dan's voice cracked over her increasingly hysterical rant like a whip. 'That's enough! You're talking nonsense.'

'It's *not* nonsense!' she argued fiercely. 'How could you have let her move into my home after all the trouble she's caused? Didn't you read my note? It's all her fault. Everything is Sara's fault.'

'Ah, yes. The note,' Dan said, and Sara seemed to be the only one who noticed a strange edge to his voice.

'You mentioned it before,' he continued. 'Remind me, when did you write it and where did you put it?'

'I wrote it the afternoon I took the tablets, of course, and I put it on my bedside cabinet, where you'd see it when you came in... And I'm so sorry for doing that to you, but if you'd read the letter you would know how desperate I was...that I just couldn't cope any more with Sara wanting to keep the baby and...'

'Shh, sweetheart,' Audrey soothed, reaching for one of her daughter's flailing arms. 'It can't be good for you to get in such a state. Perhaps it would be better…' She turned with a scowl on her face to send a meaningful glance between Sara and the door.

Sara hadn't known whether to leave so that her sister didn't upset herself any more, but Dan had already drawn the wheelchair fully into the room and shut the door for some semblance of privacy so she was completely trapped when he drew a slightly crumpled piece of paper out of his jacket pocket.

'I take it that this is the letter you're talking about?' he said, and Sara felt sick when she saw the malice in Zara's glance across at her.

'You found it!' she exclaimed. 'So now you know exactly—'

'"My darling Danny,"' he read flatly, interrupting her without an apparent qualm. '"I can't bear it any more. You know how hard we tried to have a baby and what a wrench it was for me to have to have my sister being a surrogate for us. I know that she's always wanted you for herself and I'm just so afraid that she's going to steal our precious baby and there's nothing I can do about it. I just can't bear it any more, Your loving Zara."'

Sara felt the blood drain from her face then flood back in a scalding blush when he read the note for all to hear. Didn't he realise how humiliating it was for her to have her unrequited love spoken about like that? Didn't he realise that, even if she hadn't loved him, she would still have loved the children she was carrying because they were an intrinsic part of her?

And the letter was a complete lie because even though

she desperately wished that she was carrying Dan's babies for the two of them, there was no way that she would have broken her promise to him to give him the family he wanted. He was going to be a wonderful father and Audrey would spoil her grandchildren at every opportunity and provide the feminine touch that Zara would probably be too busy for.

She really didn't need all this extra emotional stress, to say nothing of the embarrassment of having her private feelings paraded for all, not when all the pregnancy books advised calm and serenity for the sake of the baby. After all, she was still recovering from her injuries and had, admittedly voluntarily, just gone through the exertions of moving out of his flat and back into her own.

And going from mind-blowing topics to the merely petty, there was the fact that she wasn't certain her smart-enough-for-work trousers would ever recover from her decision to come all the way down four flights of stairs on her bottom.

'Look at her face!' Zara demanded shrilly, pointing straight at Sara. 'At least she has the honesty to look guilty.'

With everyone's eyes directed at her, Sara had felt the heat of embarrassment flooding into her face. She was unused to being the centre of attention at any time, least of all when she was in the same room as her twin.

She hated what Zara was doing to her but she had known for far too many years that there was no point protesting her innocence. Zara's position as everybody's favourite was unassailable. The thing that hurt worst was the fact that Dan was privy to all Zara's spiteful lies. At least in the past it had been kept within the family.

'You ask her, Danny,' her sister demanded, with every evidence of being on the verge of tears. 'You ask her if she hasn't been thinking about keeping the kid for herself.'

Of course she'd been thinking about it, Sara admitted silently as she reached for the rim of the wheel to turn herself around. She was carrying the babies of the man she loved so it was obvious that she would long for the chance to bring them up with him, and there was no way she was staying in this room to allow her sister to make something shameful about a normal human response.

'Sara, stay,' Dan said in a low voice, his lean fingers resting on her wrist to dissuade her from opening the door. 'Please?'

There was something in those amazing green eyes that told her she could trust him, that he wasn't asking her to stay to have more humiliation heaped on her head. And even though she had no idea where this dreadful conversation was going, she knew that she *could* trust him, implicitly.

She missed the warmth of his touch when he took his hand away, but then he reached into his pocket again and pulled out a plastic bag.

Walking over to the side of Zara's bed, he tipped out a piece of plastic onto her lap.

'Do you know what that is?' he asked in a quiet conversational tone.

Sara almost gave herself away with a gasp of surprise. The last time she'd seen a piece of plastic like that had been in the garage when they'd been asking about the damage to Zara's car.

'Of course I don't know what it is,' she said with a dismissive shrug. 'It's just a bit of scrap plastic.'

'Actually, it's a bit more than that,' he said with a noticeably sharper edge to his voice as he retrieved it and put it back in the bag, without touching it with his fingers. 'It's part of the light from your BMW—the one you broke when you ran your sister down and left her lying in a side street, not caring whether she was alive or dead.'

'That's a lie!' Audrey gasped, clearly shocked out of her unaccustomed bystander's role. 'That's a wicked, wicked lie. Danny, why are you doing this to Zara? She's your wife and she's ill. You should be supporting her, not spouting this ridiculous nonsense that Sara's been feeding you.'

'Audrey—' Dan said forcefully, trying to break into her tirade.

'*I* know why you're doing it,' she continued, condemnation in every stiff inch of her. 'The two of you have got your heads together and made the whole thing up to cover up the fact that you've got a thing going between you. *You're* an adulterer and *she's* no better than a…'

'Mrs Walker,' Dan barked, apparently reverting to formality as nothing else seemed to be getting through. 'If you dare say one derogatory word against Sara, I shall assume you're hysterical and slap you.'

'What?' Her eyes and mouth were wide with shock but she must have seen something in his face that made her believe he would do what he'd threatened because she subsided ungracefully into the chair on the other side of Zara's bed.

'As I was saying,' Dan continued, apparently calm

again, but from her position Sara could tell from the way
his veins were distended that his anger must have sent his
blood pressure up. She would have to suggest that he have
it checked, but for now she was still amazed that he would
have sided with her against the rest of her family. No one
had ever done that before. 'Unfortunately, it's the truth. I
took that piece of plastic from the BMW and gave it to the
police because I saw that there were fibres caught in it.
Their forensic labs have confirmed that they were strands
of top-quality vicuna and that they were an absolute match
for the fibres in Sara's coat—the one you gave to her and
that she was wearing when you knocked her down.'

There were several seconds of horrified silence at the
end of his recitation and Sara almost felt sorry for her
parents when she saw the way they were staring at their
beloved daughter…almost as if they didn't recognise
her any more…as if she'd suddenly grown a second
head, or something.

'All right!' Zara snapped. 'So it all went a lot further
than I expected, but I *still* didn't get what I wanted, and
that was to get rid of the kid.'

It was all too much for her mother to cope with and she
burst into noisy tears, unwilling even to be consoled by
her husband.

'Why did you have to go poking around? Why couldn't
you just leave it alone? After all, bones heal and she's still
carrying your precious baby… Oh, I'm sorry, it's *babies*,
isn't it? There's two of the ghastly ankle-biters in there,
gradually bloating her body until she's going to look like a
hippo.'

'Why, Zara?' Frank demanded, obviously completely confused. 'What went wrong? You seemed so happy until you couldn't have children, but then Sara offered—'

'Sara didn't offer,' she interrupted rudely. 'Mum virtually blackmailed her into it because I said I couldn't get pregnant.'

'Well, there was very little likelihood that you'd be able to while you were taking the Pill,' Dan supplied dryly.

Zara blinked, as though surprised that he knew that she'd been lying to him, but he was already moving on. 'What I don't understand is why you went through the whole pantomime in the first place.'

'Typical man!' she scoffed, tossing her head in a well-practised move that sent her hair tumbling over one shoulder. 'It's obvious. It was all a game, just a bit of fun seeing how easy it was to take you away from Sara, especially when I could tell that she had already fallen head over heels for you. *I* didn't love you—never really wanted you, if you want the truth—I certainly never had any real intention of going as far as marriage.'

Her mother gave a little whimper of distress but that only seemed to enrage Zara further and she turned her fury on her parents. 'If you two hadn't been so bloody eager to put on the big flashy fairy-tale wedding, none of this would have happened. I'm a successful model and there's a possibility that I might get a part in a Hollywood film. The last thing I want is to be stuck at home, nothing more than a housewife with two brats.'

'So, let me get this right,' Dan said icily. 'Everything you've done—married me, almost killed your sister because she's pregnant with the child you said you wanted, *and* taken an overdose of drugs—which, by the way, you carefully timed so that, if I hadn't been taking care of Sara, I would have found you before they'd had time to get into your system—*all* of that is somebody else's fault and beautiful Princess Zara is the innocent victim? I think not.'

He took a step closer so that he positively loomed over her and his words had the precision of surgical steel.

'The police are waiting for me to report back before they charge you with the attempted murder of your sister and her unborn children. If you're found guilty…which I hardly think is in doubt…you can expect to be sentenced to a minimum of twelve years in prison, but it's more likely to be eighteen years.'

'Eighteen years!' Audrey wailed, but Zara didn't say a word, at last speechless now that she'd been confronted with the probable consequences of her actions. 'She didn't mean to do it.' Audrey turned pleading eyes on Sara, as ever protective of her favourite daughter. 'You couldn't possibly send your own twin to prison.'

'I really didn't mean to do it,' Zara said suddenly, the subdued tone of her voice and the ghastly pallor of her skin telling Sara that perhaps she really was telling the truth this time. 'I've had a couple of photo shoots on the West Coast—of America,' she added, in case they weren't following. 'And when the possibility of this acting job came up and then became a probability, I suddenly felt trapped because the baby…*babies*,' she corrected herself, 'weren't due until a couple of weeks after filming's due to begin.'

'That still doesn't explain why you would decide to

run your sister over. Why on earth would you want to kill her?'

'Why? Because she's too bloody perfect,' she snarled. 'She got all the brains in the family and just sailed through school and medical training, *and* she got the beauty as well.'

'That's why you did this,' Sara murmured as she traced her original scar, the one Zara had given her so many years ago. 'I thought it was because you wanted people to be able to tell us apart. I never dreamed it was because you hated me.'

'No!' It was the first time that her sister hadn't rushed to claim that it had been an accident and the fact that her first instinct had been to deny that she hated Sara thawed something deep inside her that had been frozen for a very long time. 'Oh, everything just got so muddled in my head, probably because of the tablets one of my friends gave me.'

'Tablets?' Dan demanded instantly. 'What tablets? Where did you get them from?'

'My friend said she got them from America, on the internet. They call them designer drugs. They're gone now,' she added hastily. 'I flushed them when I got back to the flat after I…after…' She shook her head and started to shed what were probably the first genuine tears in years. 'My friend and I were high on them when she said my only option was to get rid of the baby, then I wouldn't have to be stuck in England, and my head was so messed up that it seemed to make perfect sense. Then, when I was driving towards Sara in that lane and her first thought was to save the baby…I was just so angry that she always…always did

the *right* thing that I…that I aimed straight at her and…
Oh, God, I'm sorry, Sara,' she gasped. 'And I'm just so glad
that I didn't…didn't k-kill you…'

One part of Sara's brain must have been registering the
changing figures on the electronic monitors because
somehow she wasn't in the least surprised when Dan
reached for her sister's wrist to feel for himself just how
fast her pulse was beating.

'What's wrong?' Audrey demanded. 'What's the matter
with Zara?'

'Probably nothing more than too much stress in the last
half-hour,' he said soothingly.

'It's not her liver, is it?' her father suggested fearfully.
'It's not packing up completely, is it?'

'It's unlikely that it will pack up.' This time his tone was
reassuring. 'That was one of the reasons why I started in-
vestigating Sara's accident, because if it had been Zara responsible for running her over, then it meant the drugs
probably hadn't been in her system long enough to do
serious permanent damage.'

'So, what's the matter now?' That was her mother again,
holding onto Zara's hand as though it was a lifeline. 'Why
are the monitors peeping and pinging like that?'

That, in far more clinical terms, was Mr Shah's first
question when he appeared in the doorway a few seconds
later, obviously alerted by the member of staff at the unit's
central monitoring station.

'Her pulse and respiration were probably elevated by a
family discussion,' Dan said blandly.

'In that case, I think I will have to ask you to leave,'

the consultant said formally. 'There has been a slight improvement in my patient's condition and I don't want anything to reverse it. Please, if you could return at the next visiting hour?'

Her mother obviously knew from the man's quiet air of command that there was no point trying to persuade him to change his mind and she bade her daughter a tearful good bye before leaving the room with her husband's arm supportively around her shoulders.

She was so wrapped up in her misery that she barely glanced in Sara's direction, so nothing had changed there.

'You, too, please,' Mr Shah said to Dan and Sara. 'I know you are both doctors in this hospital so you will know how important proper rest is for a body when it is recuperating.'

'Of course, sir,' Dan said respectfully, and walked round behind Sara to take charge of the handles of her wheelchair.

At the last moment before she left the room, Sara glanced back over her shoulder to meet the golden hazel eyes that were the absolute double of her own.

'The authorities will *not* be informed,' she said cryptically, and saw from the dawning relief on her sister's face that she had understood what Sara was trying to tell her.

'I take that you meant you won't be preferring charges against your sister,' Dan said in a low voice meant for her ears alone.

'I'm presuming that you didn't give those authorities enough information to work out what happened with the car?' she countered.

'So you're just going to let her get away with it?' he asked in a voice that was as unreadable as the face in front of her in the lift.

'As there was no permanent damage done...' she agreed, very conscious that they had a captive audience. 'The penalty seems out of proportion.'

'I wouldn't know,' he admitted with a fleeting glimpse of a grin. 'I made that bit up.'

Sara nearly choked trying to subdue her sudden laughter. 'Remind me not to play poker with you.'

'Shame,' he teased as he pushed her across the reception area. 'I was thinking of suggesting a game after we eat tonight. What do you think?'

What she thought was that she'd completely forgotten to tell him that she'd moved out of his flat today.

'Um... Actually, Dan, I've moved back into my own place, so I won't be—'

'What? When?' he demanded, clearly startled, and just for a moment she tried to persuade herself that he looked disappointed, too. 'And how did you get there?'

'St George rescued me from the dragon,' she said, opting for laughter rather than tears as she suddenly realised that she had absolutely no idea where she stood with him any more.

CHAPTER EIGHT

THERE had been no mistaking the expression on Dan's face that time, Sara thought while he drove her towards her flat in complete silence. That had definitely been more than disappointment on his face, it had been hurt.

'Can you manage by yourself from here?' he asked briskly, and she suddenly realised that he had pulled up outside the front of her house.

She sighed heavily, wondering when she was ever going to get anything right.

'Dan, you saw how difficult it was for me to get into the car once I was out of the wheelchair. There are only two ways of getting up the four flights of stairs once I get in there, and that's either on my bottom the whole way or if someone helps me.'

'So why did you move back here, then?' he demanded impatiently. 'My place is eminently more suitable for someone in your position because it's got a lift.'

Unfortunately, it had far more than a lift. It had Dan living there, too, and she just couldn't cope with staying with him any longer.

'And it's Zara's place, too, and with any luck it won't be too long until she's ready to come home to it.'

'And?' Those green eyes were far too astute. Sometimes she was convinced that he could read her mind.

'And there's no way that Zara and I can live in the same flat, not after what's happened,' Sara said bluntly. 'She said she's sorry and she didn't mean to do it, but she said the same thing about this…' She pulled her hair away from her race to reveal the first scar her twin had inflicted on her so long ago. 'And she's said it over and over again until… Well, let's just say I don't really trust her because the only one who matters to Zara is Zara.'

He reached his hand out towards her and gently laid it over hers where she'd unconsciously splayed it protectively over the hard curve of her pregnancy.

'You don't trust her to be too close to the babies?' he asked, but they both knew it wasn't really a question.

He closed his eyes and drew in a deep breath then opened them again and gave a brisk nod as if he'd just come to some momentous decision.

Rather than telling her about it, he released his seat belt and slid out of the car, leaving her feeling strangely dissatisfied.

'Come on, then, let's get you up those stairs,' he said, and hauled her unceremoniously to her feet.

'All I can say is it's a good job you're not coming into work for a few weeks yet, or you'd have to set off the previous day to get there in time for your shift,' he teased when they finally reached the top floor.

That's what you think, she mused as she lay in bed later

that night and contemplated the prospect of weeks of sitting around, twiddling her thumbs.

'It would drive me completely mad, just staring at the walls when I could be making myself useful at work,' she continued aloud.

She tried to remember a precedent for a member of staff coming in to work a shift while they were sporting a cast and couldn't, but... 'There's that doctor who uses a crutch on that American hospital drama!' she remembered. 'She can get up a fair turn of speed on it and still manages to take care of patients.'

She gave a quiet snort of laughter, trying to imagine herself using an actress in a fictional hospital to argue her case for an early return to work.

'Well, that character may be fiction but I'm not. This is reality and the hospital is chronically short of staff. And even if I have to put up with weeks of being stuck in minors until the cast comes off, that's what I'm going to do.'

An hour later she was still lying there wide awake, her brain going round and round the same scene, even now unable to believe that her sister could have wanted to harm the infant she was carrying. It was hard to drift off to sleep when all she could see in her mind's eye was the harsh glare of the headlights bearing down on her.

'Did I do the right thing in promising not to press charges?' she wondered aloud. 'Should I have made some sort of formal complaint so that, if at some time in the future something should happen to the babies, they'll investigate Zara first?'

That hadn't been the right thing to think about as she

was trying to sleep. She felt sick at the very thought of something or somebody hurting them.

But what would she be able to do about it once they were born and she'd handed them over? On that day she would officially become their aunt rather than their mother and would have no legal say in what happened to them.

A feeling close to panic started to fill her and for several mad moments she imagined herself grabbing her passport and slipping out of the country. There was a whole wide world out there and in almost every country there were people crying out for doctors to treat their sick and injured. Surely she would be able to find a way to support herself and the two precious lives inside her?

Then she imagined how Dan would feel, knowing that somewhere in the world there were two children bearing his genes and he'd never seen them…beyond a fuzzy ultrasound picture.

Just the idea of the man she loved gazing longingly at that image year after year was enough to bring the hot press of tears to her eyes and she knew she couldn't do it to him.

So, what was she going to do?

A strange sensation deep inside drew her attention away from that insoluble conundrum and she pressed her hand over the firm curve, remembering with a smile the way Dan had placed his hand over hers.

Oh, yes, he was going to be such a good father to this little pair. Kind and gentle and endlessly patient and…

What was that?

She froze into complete stillness and concentrated, aware that all the textbooks said it was far too soon but…

'There it is again!' she exclaimed aloud when she felt the faint fluttering, hoping it was something more than gas travelling through her gut.

When she felt it for a third time she was certain and wanted nothing more than to whoop with delight, no matter that it was pitch dark outside and everyone else in the flats was probably fast asleep.

But she couldn't just lie here in the dark and savour it all alone. She had to share the news with someone else or it wouldn't feel as if it was real. She had to speak to…

'Dan? Did I wake you?' she asked apologetically when he answered the phone.

'No. I'm in bed but I haven't gone to sleep yet. What's the problem? Is something wrong?'

'No. Nothing's wrong,' she reassured him quickly. 'It's just that I was lying there and…and…' Suddenly, it felt so wrong to be telling him such momentous news when he was on the other end of the telephone. These were *his* babies, too, and he should have been here with her to feel…

'There *is* something wrong,' he said decisively. 'I can hear you crying.'

There was the sound of a crash on the other end of the line and some muttered words that were probably unprintable, then he was back with her again.

'I'm coming over,' he announced in a don't-argue-with-me voice. 'I'll need you to drop a set of keys down to me out of a window, because you're *not* to come all the way down those stairs again.'

'Drive safely,' she said, worried about his state of mind, but he'd already broken the connection.

Suddenly, she remembered that he didn't live more than a few streets away and in that powerful car of his it would only take minutes to get there.

'Keys. Keys,' she muttered as she heaved herself out of bed, briefly registering that round about the time that she finally had her bulky cast removed it would also be the time when her pregnancy made moving about more difficult.

'So, this is what my life is going to be like for the next few months,' she grumbled, then subdued a shriek of horror when she caught sight of herself in the mirror on the back of the bathroom door.

'Talk about the wreck of the *Hesperus*,' she moaned as she dragged a brush through the tangles put there by her restlessness. At least she wasn't having to do it with her injured arm. If she'd dislocated her right shoulder she would have been strapped up and completely out of action for several weeks yet.

And as for what she was wearing…this old T-shirt hadn't just seen better days, it had seen better years, and was so worn out that it really *was* translucent in places.

Before she could strip it off, she heard the deep purr of one of the more expensive makes of car outside the front of the house and her heart did a crazy little tap-dance at the knowledge that Dan had arrived.

'The keys! What did I do with…? Ah!' She pounced on them and hobbled over to the window, steadying herself against the furniture. 'Catch!' she called in a stage whisper as she lobbed them in a gentle arc towards him, then fastened the window as fast as she could and went back to changing her clothing.

He must have taken all four flights two at a time because he was already at her front door and fitting the key to the lock before she'd pulled a fresh, slightly less disreputable T-shirt on while balancing on one leg.

'Very fetching!' he teased, and she knew he'd caught sight of one of the packet of thongs she'd bought with him the morning after her accident.

'A gentleman wouldn't have looked, and if he accidentally caught sight of something he shouldn't, he certainly wouldn't have mentioned it,' she said sternly.

'Whatever made you think that I was a gentleman?' he said with one of those cheeky grins that never failed to turn her inside out, right from the first time she'd met him.

Oh, how hard it had been, day after day, forcing herself to keep a strict distance between the two of them and making herself treat him the same as all the other A and E staff.

'So, tell me,' he said as he guided her back to the side of her bed, the rumpled covers mute evidence of her lack of sleep. 'What had you so upset that you were crying?'

'I wasn't upset,' she denied, then had to blink as her eyes began to fill with tears again. 'I was lying in bed and I was resting my hand on the bump—'

'You do that a lot,' he interrupted seriously, once more resting his much longer, much broader hand over hers. 'I've seen you doing it around the department, and when you're sitting having a break you sometimes stroke your hand backwards and forwards and round and round.'

For a moment she lost the power of speech. How had he managed to see so much when she hadn't even noticed him looking?

'I'm sorry. I interrupted you,' he said, sliding his fingers between hers so that their sensitive tips were stroking her, too. And even though there was a layer of soft stretchy fabric between them, his fingers were so warm that she could feel each one of them and the tracks they made on her skin as clearly as if she'd been naked under his touch.

'You were saying that that you were lying with your hand on your bump, and…' His voice was deeper and huskier than before, almost as though he was as affected by the contact between them as she was.

'And I felt them move,' she finished in a whisper, and saw his eyes flare wide in response.

'Are you sure?' Now he was staring down at the curve that was still almost small enough to be spanned by fingers as long as his. 'Surely it's still far too early?'

'That's what I told myself,' she agreed, 'but then it happened again, and a third time and…and I thought you would want to know and…'

He drew in a shuddering breath and she was stunned to see the bright sparkle of tears gathering in his eyes.

'Oh, thank you, Sara,' he said, so softly that she almost had to lip-read the words. 'I can't tell you how much…' He shook his head, obviously moved beyond mere conversation.

'I don't know if they're still moving, but do you want to…?'. She slid her hand out from under his and lay back across her bed, leaving his much larger hand spread across her.

It was so silent in the room that she could hear the

numbers click over on the radio alarm beside the bed, so silent that both of them seemed to have forgotten to breathe while they waited for something to happen.

'What did it feel like?' he murmured so softly that it was almost as if he was afraid of frightening them, as if those tiny forms were timid wild animals.

She concentrated for a moment, recalling the movement deep inside her.

'It felt like a cross between a flutter and a squiggle,' she said in the end. 'It wasn't quite as delicate as a butterfly's wing—it was slightly too substantial for that. But it wasn't strong enough to be called a—'

'There!' he exclaimed with a look of awe on his face as he stared down at the place covered by his hand. 'Was that what you felt?'

Sara concentrated for several long seconds and was growing worried that they'd reached the end of the performance when she felt the strongest movement yet.

'Yes!' she agreed joyfully, overwhelmed to be sharing this special moment with him. 'That's exactly what I felt. What do you think?'

'What do I think?' he asked seriously, a hint of a frown drawing those straight dark eyebrows together. 'I think it's boys, because that was definitely the sort of kick that will score goals.'

'Idiot.' She chuckled, delighting in his nonsense, but when she thought he would take his hand away again, he didn't, propping himself on one elbow on the bed beside her so that he could leave it just where it was.

'I was being serious,' he said with a deliberately solemn

expression, then asked, 'What do you think they are? Identical or fraternal? Girls or boys?'

'Or one of each?' she suggested. 'I've never understood some people being adamant about the sex they want their baby to be. I've always believed that it's far more important that it arrives as healthy and as safely as possible.'

Their undemanding conversation had drifted from topic to topic, all loosely connected with pregnancy, labour and the care of newborns, and it was some time before Dan realised that Sara had fallen asleep.

For some while he lay there watching her, glad that the room was still warm enough so that he didn't need to cover her with the bedclothes just yet, not while he was enjoying looking at the changes this pregnancy was causing to her body.

She'd never been as artificially slender as Zara and the soft curves of her burgeoning breasts and the full curve of her swelling belly were so naturally sexy that he'd been hard from the moment he'd walked into her flat and caught a glimpse of that skimpy purple thong.

Oh, what a fool he'd been, to be taken in by Zara's spiteful games. How could he not have seen while he'd been reaching for the paste imitation that he'd already had a diamond within his reach? Sara wasn't just a gifted and hard-working doctor, she was also one of the most genuinely good-hearted people he'd ever met. And, unless some sort of miracle happened, he'd lost her for ever.

So you'd better make the best of this special time, then, said a stern voice inside his head, and he took the words to heart. It might be the only opportunity he ever had to spend the night with her and he wasn't going to waste a moment of it.

In the end, exhaustion got the better of him and the next thing he knew he was waking up with Sara's softly curvy form wrapped firmly in his arms as if he was never going to let her go.

'If only,' he mouthed, full of regret, and whispered a kiss over the crown of her head.

A casual glance towards her bedside cabinet brought her clock into focus and he had to stifle an oath when he saw what time it was.

He hated having to do it, but there was no way he could untangle himself from her without disturbing her sleep. Besides, her cast had been resting over one of his ankles and he didn't know whether he was even going to be able to walk on it. It felt as if the weight might have caused permanent damage to his circulation.

'Sara?' he called gently, hoping he might be able to rouse her just far enough to extricate himself. 'Sweetheart, I've got to go,' he said a little more firmly when she just tightened her hold on him. 'I'm going to be late.'

'Late?' she repeated sleepily, and blinked…then blinked again and stared at him in disbelief. 'Dan? What are you doing here?'

'You invited me. Remember?' He only meant to prompt her memory by stroking his hand over the curve of her belly but when he found himself stroking naked skin he pulled his hand away as swiftly as though he'd been burned.

'Sorry,' he muttered, mortified to feel the heat searing his cheeks as he rolled swiftly out of reach and leapt to his feet.

His shoes were scattered on the floor and his keys were…under the edge of her bed, and his brain was definitely lodged south of his belt while she was curled up in the middle of all those crumpled bedclothes like a sleepy cat.

'I'm sorry but I've got to run or I'll be late for my shift,' he apologized, and let himself swiftly out of her flat, then nearly tripped on his way down the stairs when his hormones reminded him that he'd never seen a sleepy cat with such long slender legs…even though one of them was temporarily encumbered with a clumsy cast…or wearing such an outrageous scrap of underwear.

To lessen the danger that his preoccupation might cause an accident in the early-morning traffic, he forced himself to concentrate on the evidence he'd seen of how well her injuries were healing.

It hadn't been many days since she'd cheated death by inches, but already some of the bruises were starting to fade, working their way through the colour progression that marked the body's reabsorption of the various constituents in the blood.

He'd only caught a glimpse of her shoulder and most of the injured area was still covered by the strapping that was providing stability and support while the internal damage to the structures in and around the rotator cuff were repairing.

The grazes on her arm were much better than when he'd last seen them. Then, she'd been with Rosalie, the technician, having an ultrasound to find out if the pregnancy had been compromised, and she'd looked as if she'd been flayed raw almost from wrist to elbow.

It was all scabbed over now, evidence that none of the damage had gone very deep, and within a few more days she would be left with nothing worse than a deep pink mark on her skin that would probably be completely un-detectable in a matter of weeks.

The rest of her skin had looked silky-smooth and perfect and he'd longed to explore every inch of it in great detail and...

Whoa! That sort of thinking wasn't the right way to keep his car safely on the road. For that, he needed to keep his thoughts on the straight and narrow, too, as befitted a married man.

And if *that* reminder wasn't enough to take the shine off a morning that had started so sweetly, with the mother of his unborn children wrapped so trustingly in his arms, then nothing could.

Sara was cross with herself that she hadn't remembered to set her alarm the previous night. This morning she'd intended getting up bright and early so that she could go in to the hospital to negotiate her partial return to work.

By the time she managed to get herself washed and dressed, she was going to arrive hours after the morning shift had started and was going to give the department manager grounds to doubt that she could cope with coming back to work so soon.

Ah, but she couldn't really find it in her to regret the

reason why her plans had become so disrupted. Feeling the babies move for the first time had been amazing, and it had been made even more magical when she'd been able to share it with Dan.

Waking up this morning to find that he was still with her and knowing that his body had been wrapped protectively around hers while she'd slept was a bonus she'd never expected, and she refused to feel guilty about it. To have heard that her sister had deliberately ensnared Dan purely out of spite and, worse, that she hadn't even loved him when she'd married him—the whole situation seemed an utter travesty of everything that a marriage should be.

'If he had married me…' she whispered wistfully, then gave herself a shake. '"If wishes were horses then beggars would ride," Granny Walker used to say, and I'm just wishing for the moon, too.' And nothing could come of those wishes because even though Zara might not have loved Dan, he must have loved her or he would never have proposed to and married her.

'And none of that will get this beggar a ride, but a phone call will,' she declared when she was finally as ready as she could be. She reached for her purse and the business card of her own personal knight on a white charger…or in a black cab if she really wanted to be pedantic.

'Sara! What on earth are you doing here?' called one colleague when he caught sight of her.

'You're supposed to be on sick leave, darlin', taking it easy while the rest of us soldier on,' added Sean O'Malley in his lilting Irish accent. 'Have you just come to gloat?'

Everywhere she looked there was the usual morning chaos, except it seemed even worse than usual—or was that just wishful thinking? If everyone was being rushed off their feet, would that mean that she would be welcomed with open arms or would she be seen as a liability and shown the door?

There was only one way to find out.

'Actually, Sean, I wanted to have a word with the department manager and—'

'Oh. Admin stuff,' he said dismissively. 'Well, while you're in those recently refurbished offices sitting on one of their ultra-expensive chairs, will you remind someone that they still haven't scraped the loose change together to find us any replacement staff, not even part-timers? And we're already two and a half doctors down. It's getting beyond a joke.'

The staff in the human resources office reminded Sara of an ants' nest that had just been given a vigorous stir with a big stick.

Not that any of them seemed to be moving with the same innate sense of purpose that you'd find among ants. In fact, as far as she could tell, there was interminable duplication of effort going on while they seemed to concentrate most of their efforts on finding reasons why things *couldn't* be done.

'Have you found the new staff for A and E yet?' she asked sweetly, then gave the nest a deliberate extra stir. 'I heard a rumour that if you don't find them soon, it may have to be shut down because it's dangerously understaffed, and all the patients will be diverted to other hospitals. Doesn't the hospital get a massive fine if that happens?'

By the time she was shown in for her 'chat' with one of the more senior members of the department, the rumour she'd started seemed to have taken on a life of its own.

'Have you any idea exactly how long you're going to need to be on sick leave?' the man asked from behind a desk that was laden with piles of paperwork nearly tall enough to hide behind.

'That's what I wanted to talk about,' she said brightly. 'The only thing wrong with me is this cast on my leg.' After all, the strapping on her shoulder was invisible under her clothing. 'And the wheelchair is only for show and to give my arms a rest from using crutches.'

It was such a long way from the truth that she almost expected to feel the searing heat of a thunderbolt from on high, but what she got instead was an administrator almost grovelling at her feet when she offered to pitch in to do an hour or two in minors to help clear the backlog. There was absolutely no mention of health and safety regulations, at least not in relation to her own fitness to work. The poor man seemed far more worried about the national disgrace that would ensue if his accident department was summarily shut down due to lack of staff.

'What on earth are you doing here?' Dan growled when he finally had a moment free to get into minors.

All morning he'd been regaled with one after another of his colleagues telling him how good it was to see Sara looking so well, and what a good job she was doing, and what a clever idea it was to have her ploughing her way through all that time-consuming debriding of wounds and painstaking stitchery, leaving the more mobile staff to do the rest of the work in the department.

'You should be at home, in bed.' And with that one sentence there was only one thing that she could think about, and she hardly needed to see the way those green eyes of his darkened with awareness to know he was thinking exactly the same thing.

'Ah…it's purely a temporary measure,' she finally managed to say. 'Someone said that they might be forced to close the department if they didn't find a few more staff—health and safety or something—and you know what chaos it causes when you have new staff who haven't a clue where anything is or how our system works…'

Enough! she ordered herself. Don't babble! Just because you can't stop thinking about the way his face lit up when he felt the babies move, and how it felt to have his arms wrapped around you…none of that means that you have to develop verbal diarrhoea.

For just a moment the way he looked at her made her think that he was going to say something of a personal nature but then he shook his head and gave a sigh of resignation.

'Don't get overtired,' he said softly, and she knew his concern was genuine.

'Don't worry, I won't do anything to risk the babies,' she reassured him. 'They've had enough trauma already.'

She was tired by the end of the day but it was a good tiredness that came from doing a worthwhile job to the best of her ability, and just before Dan appeared to offer her a lift back to her flat, she was given official permission to turn up the next day, too, so the precedent was set.

'I'm still not sure that you should be doing it,' Dan grumbled as he steered around the road that circled the whole of the hospital grounds and aimed for the exit. 'You're entitled to paid sick leave.'

'I know I am, but I really don't see the point of being paid to go mad when I can make myself useful. Go on, admit it. It worked well today, having me restricted to the needlework department. I already know the system and the staff, and everybody's been willing to help me, doing things like fetching more supplies.'

He stopped arguing after that, obviously deciding that there was little point as she had permission, and she was grateful that he would never know the real reason why she'd wanted so much to come back to work so ridiculously early.

'Because that's the only place where I can legitimately spend time with Dan,' she whispered as she watched from her window while he climbed back into his car and drove away.

She'd only had to see the longing on his face when he'd looked at her belly just a few minutes ago to know that he was yearning to feel the babies move again…probably as much as she did. But their situation as nothing more than the genetic parents of those babies made the relationship between them too strained for such intimacy to take place again.

As for the possibility that Dan would wrap her in his arms again and cradle her all night long, she may as well cry for the moon.

CHAPTER NINE

THE wretched woman was driving him mad.

It wasn't enough that she was back at work long before she should have been, and that the whole of the rest of the department had welcomed her with open arms, or that she'd made herself virtually indispensable as she'd beavered away in minors.

Her bright idea was almost single-handedly responsible for the 'new initiative' that the bean-counters had come up with. This meant allocating one member of the medical team per shift to do exactly what Sara had been doing—clearing the department of the vast numbers of niggling minor injuries that, in the strict rotation of normal triage, would ordinarily clog the place up and ruin the hospital's performance figures.

If he were honest, he would have to admit that the new organisation had certainly raised morale among the A and E staff, with far fewer instances of abuse hurled at them from members of the public who had been forced to wait unacceptable hours before there had been anyone free to sort them out.

Not that their department manager was going to allow medical protocols to be buried by upper-echelon diktats. He was far too experienced a man not to know that there were times when victims brought in with major injuries took absolute priority over everything else, and he wouldn't have it any other way.

No, the thing that was driving him completely off his head was the careful distance that she'd been keeping between the two of them ever since that morning when he'd woken up in her bed.

It felt as if he'd been trying to speak to her for weeks but there was never a moment when she was alone. Each time he'd had a moment to go looking for her she'd either been with a patient or in the staffroom surrounded by other colleagues willingly fetching and carrying drinks or food for her, or asking about the progress of the pregnancy, or, worst of all, putting their hands on the rapidly swelling bump to feel the increasingly visible movement inside it.

Oh, he'd been so jealous of the fact that she was letting them do that, and his only consolation was that he'd been the very first one to feel that miraculous quickening.

Zara had left the hospital now, with Mr Shah's final words—telling her that she'd been far luckier than she deserved after doing something so stupid—still ringing in her ears. She had also packed up a substantial amount of her belongings and returned to the welcoming arms of her parents to complete her convalescence. As far as the rest of the world was concerned, this was because her mother would be available to keep her company, whereas *he* would be out at work for long stretches at a time.

In reality, there was another very different reason and he needed to talk to Sara about it...

Of course he'd thought about turning up at her flat, but all the while she was wearing that cast he'd felt too guilty about the idea of forcing her to climb all those stairs in both directions to let him in. He smiled wryly when he remembered the way she'd tossed her keys out of the window to him. If he'd known then what he knew now he'd have put them in his pocket and kept them. It would have made what he was trying to do so much easier if he could just let himself into the old Victorian house and corner her in her little eyrie. Then she would *have* to listen while he explained, apologised, did whatever he had to while he tried to persuade her to give him a chance to get close to her, because only if he could get close would he be able to judge if there was a possibility she would give him a second chance.

He was very aware that time wasn't on his side as far as her pregnancy was concerned, and he had so much to achieve before that day arrived... And then the brainwave had struck and here he was, standing on her front doorstep and ringing the bell on the ground-floor flat.

'Sorry to disturb you,' he apologised when the elderly lady cautiously opened the door with the safety chain firmly in position, 'but could you let me in so that it saves Sara coming down all those stairs?'

'Why doesn't she drop her keys down to you...like she did before?' the sprightly woman asked with a definite twinkle in her eye, and when she saw his surprise gave a chuckle. 'I don't seem to need as much sleep these days, lad, and it's amazing what I see happening outside my window.'

'I wanted to surprise her,' Dan admitted, knowing that it was nothing less than the truth. Whether Sara would see it as a good surprise he had yet to find out.

'And you brought her flowers,' his inquisitor said with a nod of approval before she released the catch. 'That's always a nice touch.'

'How did you know they were here?' he asked as he brought the bunch of freesias—Sara's favourite flowers—out from behind his back.

'The rest of me might be sagging and crumbling by the minute, but my nose is still working perfectly,' she said wryly, then a look of sad reminiscence crossed her face. 'Besides, they're my favourites and I haven't been given any since my Dermot died.'

While she stepped back and pulled the door wide, it took no more than a couple of seconds to slide several stems out of the large handful he'd brought.

'My name's Dan, not Dermot, but at least it starts with the right letter,' he said with a smile as he presented her with the sweetly scented blooms, hoping that one day Sara would have such lovely memories.

'Oh!' A shaky hand came up to cover her mouth and she blinked rapidly as though fighting back tears. 'Oh, my dear boy… Thank you so much, but you didn't have to…' She bent her silvery head to sniff the perfume before looking back up at him, her eyes misty with memories. 'You tell your Sara from me that she's a lucky young woman.'

'I couldn't possibly do that,' he said, wondering if there was a chance that Sara would ever agree with her. 'It would sound far too much like boasting. I'll leave it up to you to tell her yourself.'

She was still chuckling at his nonsense when he set off up the stairs, the flowers clutched tightly in her hand.

'Dan!' Sara gasped when she opened the door to his knock and saw him standing there, obviously the last person she'd expected to see. His heart sank when he wondered if he might be the last person she *wanted* to see.

'I come bearing gifts,' he said, suddenly remembering the flowers he was in danger of strangling to death.

'Oh, thank you!' she exclaimed, and threw him a smile that seriously weakened his knees before burying her nose in the delicate blossoms.

This time there was only the slightest hesitation before she stepped back and invited him in. 'Would you like a cup of tea? I'm afraid I've only got herbal now. Caffeine-free.'

He pulled a face and she chuckled, the simple spontaneity of the sound like balm to his soul.

'I don't much like it either, but it's better for my blood pressure and therefore better for the babies, so I have to put up with it.' She turned to lead the way into her compact kitchen and he stopped in the doorway, leaning one shoulder against the frame as he watched her bustling about.

Except she didn't bustle any more, not now that her pregnancy was advancing so rapidly. Well, rapidly wasn't quite the right word, as the duration of most pregnancies was the same, give or take a week or two. What he'd meant was that the size of her bump had increased rapidly over the last few weeks, and he hadn't really noticed the extent because she'd been spending so much of her time sitting down, working in minors.

But today had been the day that her cast had finally come off, and the first day in a long time since he'd seen her in anything other than the soft drape of a shapeless uniform dress or in a tunic top that only fitted where it touched.

Since she'd come home from work, no doubt ferried by her own personal taxi driver, she'd obviously had a bath and had donned a pair of stretchy trousers that did absolutely nothing to disguise her shape and size...and she looked wonderful, so ripe and womanly and sexy and...

'Whoa, boy! Down!' he muttered under his breath, grateful that she'd turned her back on him for a moment to give him a reprieve, and he dragged his eyes away from her lest he leap on her and carry her through to her bedroom.

'What did you say?' she asked as she turned to face him again with a steaming mug in each hand.

'I was just thinking how good you're looking, Sara.' Which was at least the polite way of voicing his thoughts as he stepped aside to allow her out of the kitchen and into her cosy little sitting room.

'It's such a relief to be out of that cast, I can't tell you.' She sank gratefully onto the settee and immediately raised her legs up onto the other seat.

He could applaud her sensible decision to rest her legs but there was no way that Dan was going to sit in the chair on the other side of the fireplace. That was much too far away for his purposes.

'Hang on to this for a second,' he directed as he held out his mug to her, and she automatically took hold of the handle. 'I'll just do this…and then settle myself here,' he said as he lifted her feet and slid onto the settee beside her before lowering her feet onto his lap.

'Dan…'

'That raises your feet slightly and improves postural drainage in your legs,' he pointed out quickly, afraid that she was going to object. 'It also means that I can do this,' he added softly, as he chose one foot and began the sort of massage that he'd learned she loved back in those days before he'd been so stupid.

'Oh! Oh…that feels so good it *must* be illegal,' she groaned as he worked on each individual muscle until he'd worked all the knots out of both feet.

'Oh,' she said again when he finally stopped, and this time it was in tones of disappointment. 'It would almost be worth getting married to have my feet massaged like that every night,' she added, and completely stole his breath away.

She'd been so relaxed by the time he'd finished that he was certain she hadn't really been thinking about what she'd said, but it was too good an opportunity to pass up.

'That could be arranged,' he said seriously, his heart beating so hard that it almost felt as if it would burst out of his chest.

He felt the tension return as if he'd flicked a switch, and he regretted that he'd spoiled her moment of rest.

'Dan, that's not funny,' she said stiffly as she started to struggle up out of the settee and he put his hand on her knee to stop her for a moment.

'I didn't mean it as a joke,' he told her, and leaned down to reach into the pocket of the jacket on the floor beside the settee.

He drew a swift breath and sent up a prayer that he'd be able to find the words he needed before he handed her the envelope he'd brought with him.

'That's a decree nisi,' he told her. 'In exactly six weeks and one day after the date on that, I can apply for a decree absolute and my marriage to your sister will be over.'

Wordlessly she stared at him then dragged her eyes down to the papers she'd withdrawn from the envelope.

'So soon!' she whispered, and he knew she'd seen the date.

'After that awful scene in her room at the hospital, I went back and had a long conversation with Zara,' he explained. 'The upshot was that our divorce petition papers had already been filed with the county court before she was discharged.'

'But…I thought you had to wait years, or for one of you to be caught being unfaithful or…' She shrugged, admitting her ignorance of such matters.

'I knew as little as you before I did some research on the internet and found out that there are five criteria but the two that applied to our situation were what they call "unreasonable behaviour"—and I would definitely class trying to murder my babies as unreasonable behaviour or…'

'You didn't tell anybody what Zara did?' she interrupted urgently. 'I promised that I wasn't going to press charges but if you've put it on the divorce papers…'

'Shh! Of course I didn't,' he soothed, taking her free hand in his and lacing their fingers together. 'But that doesn't mean I didn't use the threat of it to get what I wanted—her admission that she'd been carrying on with a man over in America. The one who's going to finance the film she's been offered a part in,' he added, although that was neither here nor there to *their* situation.

'And she admitted it? To adultery?' Her eyes were scanning the papers still clutched in her hand. 'Oh, Lord, I bet Mother wasn't happy about that.'

'I think "incandescent with rage that she wasn't going to be able to hold her head up in the neighbourhood" comes closer to the mark. I went down to see your parents to tell them in person what was going on as Zara's already gone back to the States.'

'What did she say?' There was an awful fascination in the question.

'She began by trying to forbid the two of us to divorce at all. Far too scandalous.' She'd also tried to persuade him to say that *he'd* been the one to commit adultery, but he'd been completely innocent, at least in fact if not in his head and his heart. Besides, he'd wanted to be able to come to Sara with the fewest blemishes on his character possible. He'd ruined things between them once—he didn't want to risk doing it again.

'When I finally left, after convincing her that the divorce was already a done deal, she was muttering, "Adultery!" and "The shame of it!" under her breath and your father was going to pour her a large medicinal brandy.'

'Oh, Dan, I know I shouldn't laugh, but...' Gradually,

her smile faded, to be replaced by a pensive frown, and he knew her thoughts had moved on. It was only moments later that she proved him right by asking, 'So what are you going to do now?'

It was time for another swift prayer for courage.

'My plans are already made,' he said, hoping he didn't sound as nervous as he felt. 'I've got two babies due in a matter of weeks now, and I need to find someone willing to be a mother to them, someone who will protect them as fiercely as any mother lioness defends her cubs and will love them to distraction—in fact, almost as much as she loves me.'

Sara's heart felt as if it stopped completely when she heard those words, and it seemed to take for ever before it stuttered into a proper rhythm again.

Dan was going to go looking for a good mother for his babies? But they were *her* babies, too, and…

This time she didn't let him stop her from getting up. This wasn't the sort of news she could absorb while she was lolling back on her settee with her feet propped on his muscular thigh.

Too furious to stay still, she started striding backwards and forwards in the limited space in her little living room while thoughts whirled around inside her head.

How *dared* he think of finding someone else to love her babies when *she* loved them enough to die for them—had already proved it by protecting them at the risk of her own health when Zara's car had come towards her.

She knew he didn't love her…he couldn't have if he'd

chosen Zara instead…but he'd only stipulated that the woman he wanted should love him to distraction. And she did!

But how could she tell him how she felt?

At this precise moment he was still married to her sister…or at least still legally connected so that he couldn't marry anyone else…

She stopped in her tracks as a sudden thought struck her.

Perhaps that was the problem! Perhaps the fact that he'd been married to her sister was the reason why he wouldn't even consider marrying her.

She stared out of the window into the late autumn darkness, a tiny corner of her brain telling her that she should have closed the curtains to keep the heat in, and had to concede that there would be many people who would think it creepy that he could switch allegiance from one twin to the other, as though they were as easily interchangeable as a pair of identical socks.

'When, in fact, we're more like a pair of shoes,' she muttered under her breath as she began pacing again. 'Fit perfectly one way and complete agony if you put them on the wrong foot.'

Oh, but she and Dan would have been such a good fit, she mourned as her steps gradually slowed. If only she had been just a little more like her glamorous, confident sister instead of her quiet bookish self, perhaps Dan wouldn't have been so dazzled when Zara had deliberately set out to attract him. It was all too late now, she admitted with a sigh, and her feet were dragging as she started to make her way to the chair on the other side of the fireplace, too downhearted to sit next to Dan again.

'Uh-uh!' Dan shook his head as he caught her hand and pulled her back to his side. 'That's too far away when there's still so much to talk about.'

It wasn't worth fighting about so she gave in and sat down in her corner again, resigned to listening to his plans for the rest of his life then wishing him good luck.

'Are you ready now?' he asked, and used a gentle finger to turn her head to face him.

'Ready?' she repeated listlessly, her last forlorn hopes already faded to nothing.

'Ready to listen to the biggest most grovelling apology I've ever had to make in my life.'

'Apology?' She frowned. 'What have you got to apologise for? It was your marriage and it's your right to end it. It's got nothing to do with me.'

'Oh, but it does if it should have been *you* I married in the first place,' he said softly, the expression in those beautiful green eyes so sincere that her heart did that crazy stuttering thing again.

'I was a stupid, gullible idiot when Zara came on to me like that,' he said bluntly, shocking her with his brutal honesty. 'My only excuse is that she seemed to have tapped into the way I was wishing *you* felt about me—that you enjoyed my company, that you found me sexy, that you desired me—and the fact that it all came in a package that looked identical to the woman I was already attracted to seemed to completely scramble my brains and short-circuit any attempt at rational thought.'

He hesitated a moment before he picked up her hand, as though he was expecting her to refuse to let him hold it, but she couldn't refuse him, not when he wore an expression of such despair.

'I knew I was doing the wrong thing even as I was standing waiting for the ceremony to start,' he admitted in a defeated voice so at odds with the dynamic man she knew him to be. 'I saw you walk in looking like a princess, wearing that beautiful dress—'

'My grandmother's dress,' she interrupted briefly, so glad that at least he'd noticed her when she'd been looking her best. He'd seen all too much of her at the end of gruelling twelve-hour shifts.

'I knew what I was doing was wrong,' he continued, 'but I was convinced that I'd completely burned my boats with you...and, besides, I couldn't just walk out and leave Zara at the altar, so to speak. If *she* hadn't killed me, your parents would.'

'You're right there,' she agreed. 'My mother had moved heaven and earth to get everything organised so quickly. She was convinced that the reason Zara didn't want to wait was because she was pregnant.'

'Hardly!' he scoffed. 'Even when we were supposed to be "trying for a baby" she was on the Pill. Then, so I wouldn't "waste my energy", she started taking the packs consecutively so it seemed as if she never ovulated and I was never invited to go near her.'

'But...she seemed so heart-broken that she couldn't have a child with you.' This was one facet of Zara's deception that she hadn't known about before. If she had, her parents would have had no chance of browbeating her into acting as surrogate for her sister...except...

Except in her heart it had never been Zara's child she'd agreed to carry but Dan's. It had been *his* sadness she'd wanted to banish with her gift.

'Sara, there isn't really a socially acceptable way of bringing this up but…your sister and I haven't…haven't been intimate for a long time… About a year before you became pregnant or even more than that. It certainly wouldn't be as if I were leaping out of one twin's bed and into the other…'

'Leaping into…' Sara felt her eyes grow wide. She seemed to have missed part of the conversation somewhere along the line because it had almost sounded as if he was saying…as if he was asking… And to her utter shock he slid off the settee onto one knee in front of her, taking both her hands in his as he looked up into her face.

'Sara, I've had to live with the knowledge that I made an utter mess of everything when we were just starting our relationship…when I was falling in love with you. I'll never be able to forgive myself that I've completely wasted the years between when we could have been married, because it was all my own fault. Can you ever forgive me for being so stupid?'

Sara wasn't certain whether she was laughing or crying…probably both, with her emotions in such turmoil.

'Oh, Dan, if it means the difference between not having you in my life and being married to you and making a family with you…of course I can forgive you.'

She quickly realised that pulling her into his arms really wasn't a possibility with such a large bump getting in the way, but she'd loved him for so long that missing out on any more of his kisses wasn't an option.

'I want to hold you,' he murmured when they came up for air a while later, then smiled at her with that same boyish grin that had always set her pulse somersaulting. 'This settee definitely isn't big enough for the four of us.'

He helped her to her feet, the process taking far longer than it should have, in spite of the fact she no longer sported a cast, because neither of them could resist another kiss.

She was a little uncertain that this was the right time for them—after all, it hadn't been very long ago that she'd believed he was going to hunt for someone else to be a mother for his children. But she was wrapped in his arms and she knew that if she led him through to her bedroom she could trust him to be gentle with her because he loved her.

Then, almost at the foot of her bed, he hesitated, as though having serious second thoughts.

'Um, Sara…would you think me very strange if I said I'd rather we didn't make love yet?'

Disappointment had her heart plummeting to her feet. She'd honestly believed that he was just as aroused as she was, but, then, he was a handsome, fit man while she…she was a vast bulky blimp who would soon need a marquee to cover her enormous belly full of babies—definitely not anyone's idea of an ideal sex partner.

'It's not that I don't want to,' he said hurriedly, and squeezed her hand, apparently only realising that there must be something wrong when she hadn't managed to find the words to tell him she didn't mind the delay. 'You only have to look south to know that's not true.'

Her eyes followed his directions and she couldn't help blushing when she saw the evidence that he definitely found her desirable, despite her advanced pregnancy.

So why was she feeling a strange sense of relief that he wanted to take the decision out of her hands, that he wanted to wait for another time to become intimate with her? But she still had questions.

'So why don't you want to go to bed with me?' she asked, needing to hear him spell out his reasons so that she knew what she was going to have to deal with. If his time married to Zara had given him unreasonable expectations about how slim and elegant his wife was going to be…

'It just doesn't feel right to be together yet,' he explained quietly, and gave a self-deprecating shrug. 'I know it's not really logical and there isn't long to wait before I can apply for the decree absolute and I've been wanting to make love to you for so long that even my *hair* aches with it, but…'

Suddenly she realised exactly what he was saying and that she felt the same way, too.

'You mean, you don't want to make love with me until you're completely free of Zara, so that there's a…a separation between those two parts of your life and a real new start,' she suggested, and felt like the brightest pupil in the class when he smiled at her.

'Exactly,' he said with patent relief. '*Do* you mind?'

'How can I when I've just realised that I feel the same way?' she admitted. 'But I would feel more than disappointed if you were also putting an embargo on kisses and cuddles.'

'There's no embargo on those,' he reassured her as he finally guided her across to the bed and laid her down on it, quickly joining her there. 'You can have as many kisses and cuddles as you want.'

In spite of the fact that the hospital was very busy, due to a combination of increasing numbers of patients with seasonal ailments and the resulting staff shortages, the next weeks simply flew by.

Sara had shared a wry joke with Dan that almost as soon as she'd be signed off as fit to return to full-time work she would be eligible to start her maternity leave.

'And not a minute too soon,' Dan growled, when he saw how exhausted she was at the end of a full shift.

In a move that had become a daily ritual since she'd accepted his proposal, he pushed her gently in the direction of the bathroom and flipped the taps on full before he turned to help her out of her clothes. 'You've got to make allowances for the fact that you're carrying twins,' he scolded gently, his eyes already scanning her from head to foot as he searched for any external signs of problems such as pre-eclampsia.

'Nothing untoward?' she prompted when he'd finished checking, but she could already tell from his face that he'd found nothing new to worry about.

'Grab hold of me,' he directed as he offered her a hand to steady her while she climbed into the bath, but she opted to throw her arms around him and share a heartfelt kiss with him first.

Next in the ritual was a leisurely soak while he made

preparations for their evening meal, then an equally leisurely foot massage that, more often than not, resulted in
Sara falling asleep.

It was such a relaxing routine and so devoid of anything
stressful that at times she wondered if she was the only one
who was aware of the gradually building level of tension.
It was worse when they slept together, curled up on the bed
on a day off duty when he managed to persuade her to take
a nap, or latterly even in the bed when cramp and backache
made her nights misery and it was easier to have her own
personal physician close at hand to administer the relevant
massage techniques.

Finally came the day that he arrived with an even bigger
bunch of freesias and a mysterious parcel that he presented
to her with a smile from ear to ear.

CHAPTER TEN

'WHAT'S this?' Sara asked as she took in the fact that the parcel looked rather hastily wrapped...most unlike the meticulous way he'd wrapped the present they'd given to her parents when they'd visited them to announce their intended marriage. 'It's a bit early for a Christmas present. That's nearly a month away.' Although it didn't look very much like it because the paper wasn't in the least bit Christmassy.

'No, it's not for Christmas, but I'm hoping that what's in it will make this the best Christmas ever,' he said, managing to look as excited as a child on Christmas morning. 'And I hope you're not going to take for ever to unwrap it,' he added, clearly impatient for her to see what was inside. 'I can't bear it when people unpick each knot or peel off the tape.'

'Well, then, this is just for you.' She chuckled, infected by his air of excitement, grabbed hold of the wrapping paper in both hands and pulled.

He groaned as the contents of the parcel flew in two directions and he had to retrieve them one by one.

'These first,' he directed. 'I took that packet of ugly harvest festivals back and swapped them for the sexiest ones I could find,' he said with a grin, and waggled his eyebrows when she blinked at just how risqué the delicate lingerie was.

'Harvest festivals?' she repeated with warmth in her cheeks, remembering the vastly oversized knickers she'd bought to fit over her cast and then never worn.

'My grandmother used to call them that,' he said with a laugh. 'She said it was because they were so all-encompassing that they reminded her of that hymn that's always sung at harvest festivals, "All is safely gathered in".'

'Well, if *they* were harvest festivals, what are *these*?' She was almost embarrassed to look at them while he was watching for her reaction. She'd worn that thong out of sheer necessity when she'd first broken her leg, but these definitely had a different purpose if his expression was anything to go by. There was absolutely nothing utilitarian about them.

'Those are definitely Mardi Gras, or even Copacabana,' he suggested, 'and I can't wait to see you modelling them.'

The heat in his eyes was enough to send her temperature and pulse soaring and it wasn't something she was used to from Dan. While they had their agreement to wait until he was finally free of his marriage to Zara, she'd recognised that he'd been walking a torturous tightrope. On the one hand he'd been at great pains to make sure that she knew just how sexy he found her ripening body and how much he desired her while preventing the situation getting out of hand.

This, today, was so out of character that she scarcely…

'And *this* is the other "Happy Christmas" present we're going to share,' he said, more seriously this time, as he handed her the other half of the parcel. It was a bulky envelope and looked quite official…almost like…

'The decree absolute,' she whispered, hardly able to believe what she was seeing when she slid the document out. 'Oh, Dan, you're free.'

'Exactly,' he said with delight, flinging both arms around her. 'And tomorrow morning we're both going to present ourselves with all our relevant documents and information and we're going to book our wedding for twenty-one days later.'

'Twenty-one days?' she repeated, quite shocked that everything suddenly seemed to be moving so fast. 'But that's so close to Christmas and…and… Dan, you've been crossing off the days until you'd be free. Don't you want a little while to get used to the idea that you're not married to Zara before you tie yourself to—?'

'Sara, my love,' he said as he tightened his arms around her and settled her head on his shoulder, where it belonged, 'there's only one reason why I've been counting every last second until I could get this decree in my hand, and that's because I can't wait to be married to you.'

'But…'

He stopped her speaking with a hungry kiss, although that was becoming more difficult without some careful positioning as her bump grew ever larger.

'And don't you start trying to come up with all sorts of ulterior motives, such as "he's only doing it so fast because he wants to be married before the babies arrive to make sure they have his name." I can tell you categorically that, while it *would* cut down on a bit of paperwork, I'd be in just as much of a hurry to marry you if you weren't pregnant at all.'

He gave her another kiss that went a long way to convincing her just how much he desired her, then cupped her face in his hands and drew back, but only far enough for her to focus on green eyes that now blazed with all the love she could ever want. He drew in a noticeably shaky breath then declared fiercely, 'Sara, I just can't wait to be able to tell the world how I feel…that the woman I love to distraction has given me the best Christmas gift in the world and is finally my wife.'

In the end, it hadn't mattered in the least that she'd been feeling as if she was the size of a small house, because Dan had been right—all that mattered *was* that they were married at last, and there wasn't a dry eye.

With so few days to go before Christmas there was evidence everywhere from the beautiful display of scarlet and green poinsettia around the room to the fine streamers of red and green ribbon spiralling down from Sara's bouquet of Christmas roses.

Sara suspected that her mother probably hadn't been able to resist comparing this small gathering in the nearest registry office with Zara's elegant ceremony. No doubt she was regretting that neither she nor Dan had been willing to give her the chance to arrange something similar for them.

This was far more intimate and more meaningful, with just their closest friends in attendance to wish them well; and she didn't have to look much further than Sean O'Malley to guess who had suggested that they should all celebrate the unique time of year by wearing red or green.

But there was no way that even Audrey could miss the loving way Dan had ushered her into the room or the supportive arm that had encircled her throughout the proceedings.

Even the registrar had looked ecstatic when she declared them husband and wife, but that was probably because the poor woman was so relieved that she hadn't had to witness a precipitate delivery all over her brightly polished floor.

'Still, it's a bit of a shame,' Sean teased when he came up to congratulate them. 'It would have been so handy for registering the birth.'

Sara was the only one who didn't laugh.

All morning she had been feeling ominous tightenings and Dan hadn't completely been able to convince her that it was just more Braxton-Hicks' contractions. She'd been horribly certain that she would never get this far before going into labour.

'I told you it would be all right,' he murmured smugly when their little gathering had filed out of the office to make way for the next couple. He stroked a loving hand over her ivory silk-draped bump. 'I had a little word with these two in here and told them we had big plans for today, so they were to stay put just a little bit longer.'

'Dan? Sara?' said a hesitant voice behind them, and

there was Zara, looking almost unrecognisable from the sickly person Sara had last seen in a hospital bed. For just a moment the sight of her sister looking so vibrant and healthy reminded Sara all too forcibly that she must look like a hippo draped in a marquee by comparison, and her hand tightened reflexively on Dan's arm.

It only took one glance from those deep green eyes to restore her confidence that he was finally married to the twin he loved.

Standing beside Zara was a man at least twenty years her senior and not nearly as handsome as Dan, but it was obvious from the way he looked at her sister that he was completely besotted.

'This is Zach,' she said, almost shyly, and this new side to her otherwise confident sister took Sara by surprise.

'I'm the guy who's putting the finance together for Zara's film debut,' he announced in an unmistakable American accent, holding his hand out to each of them in turn. 'When she told me that her sister was getting hitched, I just had to do everything I could to make sure she was here.'

'That's very kind of you,' Sara said weakly, slightly overwhelmed by the man's ebullient personality. 'Have you been to Britain before?'

'Oh, many times,' he said with a broad smile. 'My plane could probably fly here by itself, it's been so often. So don't you worry about your sister missing out on being an aunt to those kids of yours.'

'Oh, that's very—'

'And don't you worry about anything,' he added,

dropping suddenly to a confidential tone, his shoulder turned so that neither Zara nor Dan were privy to what he was saying to her. 'First, I'm going to make sure she's fully recovered, then she's going to get her shot at stardom, but somewhere down the line I'm going to do my best to persuade her that she'd like to marry me and have some kids of her own.'

He stepped back and caught Zara's hand to tuck it in his elbow. 'Now, I know this is only a flying visit, but you just send us the pictures when these two decide to arrive and let us know when the christening is. We'll be back for it.'

Sara's last secret fear—that because she'd agreed to carry these precious babies as a surrogate for her sister, Zara might have a claim on them—had just been completely demolished.

She met Dan's eyes to ask a silent question and his smiling nod gave Sara the answer she needed.

'She'll have to come back for the christening,' she announced softly, knowing her next words would send her sister the signal that all had been forgiven, 'because she's going to be their godmother...if she wants to?'

The hug they shared was awkward but heartfelt and Zara took advantage of the closeness to whisper, 'Oh, Sara, I'm so, so sorry for everything. I was such a blind fool.'

Stepping back, she managed to find a tremulous smile. 'Rather their godmother than their mother,' she joked, but Sara caught the gleam of determination in Zach's eyes.

The next day Dan and Sara had just finished decorating their very first Christmas tree together and were about to settle down to tea when there was a phone call from someone in Human Resources.

'That's ridiculous!' Dan muttered impatiently when the call ended. 'There are some papers I've got to sign…something about insurance cover for you and the babies now we're married…and they want me to come in to do it today.'

'Today?' Sara's heart sank with disappointment. They'd had some rather interesting plans for the rest of the day and some of them involved stoking up the fire in the fireplace and just leaving the lights on the Christmas tree while they… *Later*, she reproached herself, silently. *We've got all the time in the world.*

'Well, I suppose it's good that they're getting everything sorted out now, rather than later,' she conceded. 'It shouldn't take you long, should it? We'll still have the rest of the evening…and night.'

'You needn't think you're staying here, tucked up all cosy and warm. There are some things for you to sign, too, so you'd better get something warmer than that robe on.'

Sara groaned and held her hands out so that he could help her to escape from the embrace of his blissfully comfortable settee. Unfortunately, it had never been designed for an easy exit for a woman heavily pregnant with twins.

They were just walking into Reception when Sean hailed them from the other side, his red hair a beacon in spite of all the tinsel and glitter on the enormous tree beside him.

'Hey, you two! Have you come to say hello to the gang?' he asked as he came across to kiss Sara's cheek.

'Several of them were asking how you were after I saw you at the wedding. They were complaining that haven't seen you since you started your maternity leave.'

'We've actually got to see someone in Human Resources about some paperwork,' Dan said with a grimace. 'Can you believe they phoned us on a Friday afternoon *this* close to Christmas?'

'Ah, sure they can wait a few minutes,' Sean said dismissively, beckoning them in the direction of A and E. 'The department's quite quiet at the moment so you'd better take advantage of it. By the time you've finished with the paper-pushers, we could be rushed off our feet.'

Dan and Sara both knew just how true that was, so they didn't need any more persuading, but they hadn't realised that the whole thing was a complete set-up until they walked into the staffroom to a shower of confetti and a united chorus of 'Surprise!' and found the room packed with waiting colleagues.

'They couldn't be there for the ceremony but they weren't going to miss out on the reception, even if they had to lay it on for themselves,' Sean told them with a broad unrepentant grin. 'Can't have A and E missing out on anything this special!'

'And the appointment with Human Resources?' Dan asked wryly, wondering how they could have been so gullible.

'That was the only ploy we could think of to get you out of your love nest,' Sean said with a teasing wink that had Sara blushing, remembering just what they'd had planned for the rest of the day. 'Now, has anyone got a spare suture trolley somewhere? Because you look as if you need it to carry some of that weight around for you.'

The thought of Sara wheeling her bump around in front of her on one of the department's trolleys... 'Suitably decorated for Christmas, of course,' Sean had added...was enough to have them all laughing.

It wasn't until Sara and Dan had circulated for an hour, greeting each of their colleagues as one after another they managed to snatch five minutes between patients, that they finally felt they could reasonably make their farewells.

'A final toast,' Sean announced, holding up a plastic goblet of something fruity and strictly non-alcoholic that almost exactly matched the carroty colour of his hair, apparently having appointed himself master of ceremonies. 'To paraphrase an old Irish toast—May the road rise up to meet you, the rain fall soft upon your head, the wind be always at your back, and may you get to heaven half an hour before the devil knows you're gone! To the bride and groom!'

'The bride and groom,' the rest chorused amid laughter, saluting them with similarly colourful glasses, but when Sara went to raise her own glass in return, she felt a sharp pain somewhere deep inside and gasped.

'Sara? Are you all right?' Dan asked, and tightened his hand around her shoulders, instantly aware that something had happened.

The sudden cascade of fluid onto the tiled floor told him everything he needed to know.

'They're over two weeks early,' she whimpered as she gingerly sat in a wheelchair that had appeared from nowhere.

'That's par for the course with twins,' Dan said reassuringly, then bent closer to whisper in her ear. 'And it's probably due to our enthusiastically thorough consummation of our marriage. They say that the application of male hormones can set things going. And, anyway, Christmas is the perfect time for the very best gift of all...new life.'

Sara hoped it was that same delightful application of male hormones that had been responsible for an absolutely textbook-perfect delivery, with one healthily squalling little boy following the other out into the world in perfectly normal cephalic deliveries.

'Oh, Dan, look! They're beautiful!' she sobbed as she lay there in the specially subdued lighting of the delivery room with one precious dark-haired baby in each arm. 'They're identical and they look just like you.'

'You're the beautiful one,' he argued as he stroked her joyful tears away with gentle fingers. 'You're amazing, Sara Lomax, and I could never tell you how much I love you in a million years. As for you two,' he said as he turned his attention to two little boys that were so perfect that any man would be proud to be their father.

He leaned a little closer, and under the cover of the activity still going on around them said, 'I need to have a word with the two of you for spoiling things. I had big plans for your mother tonight, involving a certain black lacy thong.'

'You idiot!' Sara laughed, knowing she'd had some similar plans of her own.

She loved Dan all the more for teaching her to have confidence in herself as an attractive woman, confidence that she'd never developed when she'd always felt herself to be in Zara's shadow.

'We'll just have to remember what we had planned and save it up for later,' she suggested, her heart so full of love that it felt as if must be overflowing. 'After all, we've got the rest of our lives to love each other.'

1207/03b

MILLS & BOON®
MEDICAL™

proudly presents

Brides of Penhally Bay

Featuring Dr Nick Tremayne

A pulse-raising collection of emotional, tempting romances and heart-warming stories – devoted doctors, single fathers, Mediterranean heroes, a Sheikh and his guarded heart, royal scandals and miracle babies...

Book Two

THE ITALIAN'S NEW YEAR MARRIAGE WISH

by Sarah Morgan

On sale 5th January 2008

A COLLECTION TO TREASURE FOREVER!
One book available every month

MILLS & BOON

MEDICAL

Proudly presents

Brides of Penhally Bay

*A pulse-raising collection of emotional,
tempting romances and heart-warming stories by
bestselling Mills & Boon Medical™ authors.*

January 2008
The Italian's New-Year Marriage Wish
by Sarah Morgan

Enjoy some much-needed winter warmth with
gorgeous Italian doctor Marcus Avanti.

February 2008
The Doctor's Bride By Sunrise
by Josie Metcalfe

Then join Adam and Maggie on a 24-hour rescue mission
where romance begins to blossom as the sun starts to set.

March 2008
The Surgeon's Fatherhood Surprise
by Jennifer Taylor

Single dad Jack Tremayne finds a mother for his
little boy – and a bride for himself.

*Let us whisk you away to an idyllic Cornish town –
a place where hearts are made whole*

COLLECT ALL 12 BOOKS!

100 Reasons to Celebrate

2008 is a very special year as we celebrate Mills and Boon's Centenary.

Each month throughout the year there will be something new and exciting to mark the centenary, so watch for your favourite authors, captivating new stories, special limited edition collections...and more!

FREE!

4 Books
and a surprise gift!

We would like to take this opportunity to thank you for reading this Mills & Boon® book by offering you the chance to take FOUR more specially selected titles from the Medical™ series absolutely FREE! We're also making this offer to introduce you to the benefits of the Mills & Boon® Reader Service™—

- ★ FREE home delivery
- ★ FREE gifts and competitions
- ★ FREE monthly Newsletter
- ★ Exclusive Reader Service offers
- ★ Books available before they're in the shops

Accepting these FREE books and gift places you under no obligation to buy, you may cancel at any time, even after receiving your free shipment. Simply complete your details below and return the entire page to the address below. You don't even need a stamp!

YES! Please send me 4 free Medical books and a surprise gift. I understand that unless you hear from me, I will receive 6 superb new titles every month for just £2.89 each, postage and packing free. I am under no obligation to purchase any books and may cancel my subscription at any time. The free books and gift will be mine to keep in any case.

M7ZEF

Ms/Mrs/Miss/Mr .... Initials ....

Surname .... BLOCK CAPITALS PLEASE

Address ....

....

.... Postcode ....

Send this whole page to:
UK: FREEPOST CN81, Croydon, CR9 3WZ

Offer valid in UK only and is not available to current Mills & Boon® Reader Service™ subscribers to this series. Overseas and Eire please write for details. We reserve the right to refuse an application and applicants must be aged 18 years or over. Only one application per household. Terms and prices subject to change without notice. Offer expires 28th February 2008. As a result of this application, you may receive offers from Harlequin Mills & Boon and other carefully selected companies. If you would prefer not to share in this opportunity please write to The Data Manager, PO Box 676, Richmond, TW9 1WU.